# "Now tell me, Katrina...

"You will be at Rose Cottage until you start work again in September?"

"Oh, yes. Do you want to send another patient to stay with me?"

"No. I want you to be there, and free, so that whenever I can manage it, I can come and see you."

"See me? Why?"

"I've fallen in love with you, but you don't feel the same about me yet."

When she would have spoken, Simon said, "No, don't say anything, just bear it in mind." He spoke in a casual voice, then he added, "You won't mind if I just turn up from time to time?"

Katrina ~~~~~~~~~~~~~~~~~~~~~~~~~~~~~~~~~, I
shan~~~~~~~~~~~~~~

### WHITE WEDDINGS

*True love is worth waiting for...*

Dear Reader,

Welcome to the latest in our miniseries, WHITE WEDDINGS.

Everyone loves a wedding, with all the excitement of the big day: bedecked bridesmaids, festive flowers, a bit of bubbly and all the emotions of the happy couple exchanging vows.... Some of your favorite Harlequin Romance® authors bring you all this and more in a special selection of stories.

You'll meet blushing brides and gorgeous grooms, all with one thing in common: for better or worse, they're determined the bride should wear white on her wedding day...which means keeping passions in check!

Happy Reading!

*The Editors*

# An Innocent Bride
## Betty Neels

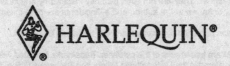

TORONTO • NEW YORK • LONDON
AMSTERDAM • PARIS • SYDNEY • HAMBURG
STOCKHOLM • ATHENS • TOKYO • MILAN • MADRID
PRAGUE • WARSAW • BUDAPEST • AUCKLAND

ISBN 0-373-03577-2

AN INNOCENT BRIDE

First North American Publication 1999.

Printed in U.S.A.

# CHAPTER ONE

THE road was narrow, high-hedged and overshadowed by trees, and, like so many English country lanes, it wound its way in a series of haphazard curves through the quiet countryside, free of traffic and pleasantly warm in the sunshine of a spring morning.

The man behind the wheel of the dark grey Bentley drove unhurriedly, enjoying the peace and quiet, reflecting that there were still quiet corners of rural England which one came upon by chance. There had been no village for some miles, and the last of the solitary cottages along the road he had passed a mile back; there had been no cars... As he thought that a motorbike came round the next curve, travelling fast and in the middle of the road, flashing past the Bentley with inches to spare, just missing it.

The driver of the Bentley swore quietly as he took the next bend in the road, to slide to a halt and get out of his car. The contents of a shopping basket were strewn across the road, a bicycle, no longer recognisable as such, was tossed to one side of the verge, and sitting near it was a girl.

She appeared unhurt but in a fine temper.

'That idiot—did you see him? On the wrong side of the road, driving like a maniac.'

The man, walking towards her, thought what a splendid creature she was: a big girl, with quantities of dark brown hair and a face whose beauty wasn't easily forgotten.

He reached her side, a giant of a man, no longer young, his pale hair grey at the temples, but handsome, with a high-bridged nose and a thin, mobile mouth.

'Yes. I saw him. Are you hurt?'

He bent to look at her and saw the blood oozing from a cut on her leg.

'Stay still for a moment; I'll fetch my bag.'

When he returned she said, 'You're a doctor? A fortunate meeting.'

He was gently cleaning the wound. 'Indeed, yes, but in hardly fortunate circumstances. This will need your doctor's attention. Where else are you hurt? You weren't knocked out?'

'No. I'm a bit sore here and there.'

'The best thing is for me to drive you to your home and get your own doctor to see you. You live near here?'

'About a mile down the road. Rose Cottage—it's on the left-hand side, and another half-mile or so to the village.'

He had bandaged her leg, cleaned the scratches on her arms and legs and brushed the bits and pieces from her hair. 'You will have some nasty bruises,' he told her. He closed his bag, bent and picked her up without apparent effort, and carried her across to his car.

As he settled her in the seat she said worriedly, 'You shouldn't have done that. I'm heavy.'

She wasn't altogether pleased when he said casually, 'But you're a big girl, aren't you?'

He smiled at her. He had a nice smile, kind and

at the same time impersonal. And it was quite true; she *was* a big girl. She sat, on the edge of tears now, watching him gather up the contents of her shopping basket and then pick up the mangled wreck of her bike and put it tidily on the grass verge. The sight of it was too much, and tears were trickling down her dirty cheeks when he got into the car beside her.

He took a quick look, offered a very large, very white handkerchief, and said in a voice as kind and impersonal as his smile, 'You'll feel better once you've had a good cry. There's nothing like it for relieving the feelings.'

He sat patiently while she sobbed and snuffled, then finally mopped her face, blew her nose and muttered, 'I'll wash your hanky and send it to you.' She looked at him from a blotchy and still beautiful face. 'My name's Gibbs—Katrina Gibbs.'

He shook the hand she held out. 'Simon Glenville. Is there anyone at home to look after you?'

'Well, no, but there will be soon—around one o'clock.'

He picked up the car phone. 'I'll ring the police and your doctor. You shouldn't be alone until there is someone to keep an eye on you.'

He was already talking into the phone. 'The police will be along shortly. Now, your doctor's name—do you know his number?'

'Yes. He has a morning surgery in the village; he's there three days a week. He'll be there today.'

She hardly listened when he phoned again, for she was suddenly tired and sleepy. Shock, she supposed; she would be all right once she was home—a cup of tea and perhaps half an hour's nap on her bed...

Rose Cottage was no more than a few minutes'

drive. It was small, with red brick walls and a rather shabby thatched roof. It stood sideways on to the road, and a wooden gate opened onto a brick path leading to its front door, solid under the thatch of the porch.

Dr Glenville stopped the car and got out. He said briefly, 'Stay there—have you a key to the door?'

'On the left-hand side there's a narrow ledge above the door...'

The key was large and heavy; Dr Glenville reflected that it was certainly too cumbersome to carry around in a woman's handbag as he opened the door. It gave directly onto the living room, which was small and rather overcrowded with furniture. A half-open door ahead of him gave him a glimpse of the kitchen beyond. There were two other doors too, so he opened the one nearest to him—another small room, the dining room presumably—and when he lifted the latch of the other door he found a narrow curved stair.

He went back to the car, opened Katrina's door and lifted her out.

'I can walk.'

'Better not until your doctor has had a look at you.'

As he thrust back the stairs door with a foot Katrina said urgently, 'You can't carry me up.'

She could have saved her breath. He didn't reply, and on the tiny landing above, still breathing easily, he asked, 'Which door?'

'On the right.' She added sharply, 'Do put me down...'

He didn't reply to that either, but laid her tidily on the narrow bed in the little room, took off her sandals and covered her with the patchwork quilt folded across its foot.

'Lie still and close your eyes,' he said, and at the thump on the door knocker he said, 'That will be the police or your doctor. I'll be back.'

'This is ridiculous,' said Katrina peevishly, but she closed her eyes and was asleep before he had reached the bottom of the stairs.

It was the police—at least, a constable, who was rather stout, with a cheerful round face, his bike leaning against the hedge by the gate. 'Had a message,' he observed, eyeing the doctor. 'I live in the village. I'm to have a look and see what's amiss. Miss Katrina's not hurt?'

The doctor held out a hand. 'Dr Glenville. I found Miss—er—Katrina in the road. A motorbike knocked her over, smashed her bicycle to bits, I'm afraid. I've phoned her doctor—she's resting on her bed. I expect you need a statement, but could it wait until she's been examined? She's rather shocked, and has been bruised and cut.'

'You saw the accident, sir?'

'No, but the motorbike missed me by inches coming round the bend, and I found the young lady sitting in the road. A mile back.'

'I'd best go and take a look. You didn't get the number, I suppose?'

'No. He was going at speed. I had to move the bike to the side of the road in case it caused a further accident.'

'You'll be here, sir?'

'Yes, I'll stay until her doctor gets here. You'll want a statement from me, won't you?'

'I'll go and take a look right away and send in a report.'

The doctor went to his car, unlocked the boot, took his case into the cottage and went into the kitchen. He supposed that he had better stay until whoever it was who would be back at one o'clock returned. He was in no great hurry to get home, and the girl shouldn't be left alone.

He prowled around the kitchen, which was almost as large as the living room, with a tiled floor and cheerful wallpaper. There was a door leading to a long garden with a small window beside it. It was open and sitting beside it, composed and dignified, was a small black and white cat.

The doctor tickled it under its chin and, rightly interpreting its fixed stare, he found a saucer, the milk in the slip of a pantry, and offered it.

The cat scoffed it daintily, got down from the window and walked out of the kitchen and through the open door to the stairs, and the doctor, raised by a loving mother and an old-fashioned nanny, put the milk back where he had found it, washed the saucer and folded the teacloth tidily over its rail. Childhood teachings don't die easily.

Footsteps coming up the garden path sent him to the door. The man about to enter was middle-aged, grey-haired, with a long thin face and a stoop. He said at once, 'Dr Glenville?' He held out a hand. 'Peters—thank heaven you were able to help Katrina. Is she upstairs?'

'Yes. The village constable came; he's gone to take a look round. I'll wait here for a bit, shall I?'

'I'd be obliged if you could. Did you form any opinion? Nothing serious?'

'It seems not, but I haven't examined her—just bandaged a cut on her leg and made sure that she hadn't been knocked out.'

Dr Peters nodded. 'I'll go on up.'

Presently he came downstairs again and joined Dr Glenville sitting on the wooden bench outside the door. 'I can't find much wrong—she tells me that she didn't lose consciousness at all. She's a healthy young woman; I don't think there's much harm done. All the same, I don't like to leave her on her own. She needs to rest for an hour or so, don't you agree? Knowing Katrina, she is quite capable, once our backs are turned, of coming downstairs to dig the garden or Hoover the house. She lives with her aunt, Miss Thirza Gibbs, who has gone into Warminster to see her dentist. Won't be back until the bus gets in round one o'clock.' He frowned. 'I wonder if the vicar's wife would pop over?'

'If it is of any help, I will stay,' said Dr Glenville, and wondered as he said it why on earth he had suggested it. 'I'm on my way back to town, but the rest of the day is my own.' He added, 'I have beds at St Aldrick's, so I have rooms in town, but I live at Wherwell.'

Dr Peters said, 'St Aldrick's's—you're the chap who wrote that article in the *Lancet*—the haematologist. I'm delighted to have met you, though I would wish for a more sociable occasion. But can you spare the time?'

'Certainly I can. Do you wish me to say anything to the young lady's aunt?'

'Miss Thirza? Would you? And tell her that I'll call in later today or tomorrow morning.' He smiled a little. 'She is a very forthright person—so, for that matter, is Katrina.'

Left on his own, the doctor trod upstairs, paused at the open door to ask if he might go in and crossed to the bed.

'Dr Peters has gone, but I'll stay until your aunt gets back. Would you like a cup of tea?'

Katrina sat up in bed and regretted it; she had the beginnings of a headache. Not surprising, really, with all the fuss... 'I can't think why you're still here,' she said rudely. 'There's no need. I'm not a baby and there's nothing wrong with me at all. Do please go away. You've been most helpful, thank you.'

The doctor studied her face. 'Would you like a cup of tea?' he asked again, in the mildest of voices.

She nodded, her eyes closed. She was behaving badly; she opened her eyes, anxious to apologise, but he had gone.

The doctor pottered round the kitchen looking for things while the kettle boiled. It was a pleasant little room, with cheerful curtains at the window, a small table against one wall and two chairs. The cooking stove was old but immaculate, and the cupboards were models of tidiness. But there wasn't a great deal in them—the basic necessities, no tins or packets— and no fridge, although there was an old-fashioned pantry with stone shelves, which was very cool.

He made tea, and since the cat was staring at him in an anxious manner he looked around for its food. There were no tins, but there was a covered saucepan on the stove with what looked like some kind of stew in it. He filled a saucer and offered it, found a mug and went back upstairs. A pity that Mrs Peach couldn't see him now, he reflected—a housekeeper of the old fashioned school, she considered that no one who employed her should lift a finger while she or Peach, her husband and his houseman, were within reach.

Katrina sat up as he went in. He put the mug down, tucked a cushion behind her and offered the tea. This time he didn't go away, but sat on the edge of the bed, steadying the mug in her hands, which were shaking.

'Headache getting better?' he asked, and when she carefully nodded he added, 'Is there anything I can do while I'm here? Phone someone?'

She said bleakly, 'We haven't got a phone.' She finished the tea and felt better. 'I'm sorry to have been so rude and ungrateful.'

'It's of no consequence.'

He sounded so casual she wished she hadn't said anything. I don't like him, she reflected crossly. He's being kind and helpful and all that, but that's because he's a doctor, and it wouldn't do if he were to jump into that great car of his and drive off.

The doctor, aware of her edginess towards him, decided that, although she was one of the prettiest girls he had seen for a long time, she had a decidedly sharp tongue and had all the obstinacy of the pro-verbial mule. Probably had an unhappy love affair, he thought idly, and it's soured her. A pity.

He went back downstairs and poured himself a mug of tea, and sat drinking it with the little cat curled up on his knee. What might have been the beginnings of a friendly relationship between them had become indifference on both their parts. Now and again, going through life, one met someone with whom one was incompatible, he reflected, allowing his thoughts to wander to the work waiting for him.

Presently he went quietly upstairs again and found her asleep, her hair an untidy cloud all over the pillow, her mouth a little open. There were scratches on her cheek and there was a bruise developing on one arm. She was a big girl, but now she looked like a child. The doctor studied her at some length, wondering why she chose to live so remotely. But that was none of his business.

He went back to the kitchen and later, when he heard the gate being opened, he went to open the front door.

The lady walking briskly up the path was of an indeterminable age, very tall and thin, with a narrow face and a sharp nose, wearing a no-nonsense hat and a dateless beige coat and skirt. When she was within a yard of the doctor she asked briskly, 'And who are you, young man? I don't expect to find strangers on my doorstep. You're surely not a friend of Katrina's?'

If that was a compliment it was surely a left-handed one, thought the doctor, and he stood aside to allow Miss Thirza Gibbs to enter her home.

'No, no such thing. Your niece has had a slight accident and I happened to be the person to find her. Nothing alarming…'

'I am not easily alarmed,' said Miss Thirza Gibbs tartly. 'Kindly get to the point. Presumably she is here?'

'In her bed.' The doctor had assumed the armour plating of his profession: an impersonal courtesy leavened with a touch of bracing sympathy. 'Your niece was knocked off her bicycle by a motorcyclist who didn't stop. She has a cut on her leg, is scratched and bruised and shocked. Dr Peters has been to see her and will call again. She didn't lose consciousness.'

'Why are you here, in my house?'

He raised his eyebrows. 'Your niece is hardly in a fit condition to be left alone, Miss Gibbs. I trust that she will make a speedy recovery. Good day to you.'

Miss Gibbs went an unbecoming red. 'I'm sure it was very kind of you,' she began stiffly.

But she was stopped gently by his, 'Not at all, Miss Gibbs. Please give my best wishes to your niece.'

He got into his car and drove away, and she went into the house and then slowly climbed the stairs.

Katrina was still sound asleep and, despite her scratches and bruises, looked her usual healthy self. Her aunt went down to the kitchen, made herself a sandwich, laid a tray with bowl, plate and spoon, set soup to warm and sat down to wait. She had had a tiring morning, and her meeting with the strange man had upset her; she had always been in the habit of speaking her mind even at the expense of other people's feelings, but the man *had* been kind. She dozed off, and when she woke, half an hour later, Katrina was sitting at the table, polishing off the last of the soup.

When her aunt opened her eyes she asked, 'Has he gone? That man—he brought me home. I didn't thank him properly. You saw him?'

Miss Gibbs got up and put the kettle on, for she felt the need for a cup of tea. 'Tell me what happened, and, yes, I saw him, but only for a few minutes.'

'Well, this motorcyclist was on the wrong side of the road—on that bend by the turnip field, you know?' Katrina gave a matter-of-fact account of the whole business, because her aunt had no patience with emotional outpourings or embellished facts, and when she had finished she said, 'It must have been a great nuisance for him.'

'He is a doctor?' Miss Thirza Gibbs frowned. 'I'm afraid that I was a little brisk with him. Perhaps he gave his name to Peters, in which case it would be quite correct for us to write him a letter of thanks for his help.'

'I wouldn't bother,' said Katrina. 'I should think he's forgotten all about it by now—besides, he didn't like me.'

'Did he say so?'

'No, of course not, Aunt, but he was—' she paused, seeking the right word '—forebearing. As though he was doing his duty and found it all a bit of a bore. I didn't like him.'

'In that case,' said Miss Gibbs, 'it is fortunate that we are unlikely to see him again.'

Katrina agreed, ignoring a sneaking feeling that even if she didn't like him it might be nice to know a bit more about him.

But even if she were never to meet him again, at least she was to know more about him, for later that day Dr Peters came. Evening surgery was over, and he was on his way home, but he sat down for ten minutes, drank the tea Katrina offered him, and expressed the view that she was perfectly fit again although she would look a bit unsightly for a few days.

'This man,' said Miss Gibbs. 'Katrina tells me that he is a doctor.'

'A specialist. He's a consultant at St Aldrick's—a haematologist—a well-known one, too. He didn't tell you? Well, he's not a man to blow his own trumpet, I should imagine. Stayed for lunch, did he?'

Miss Thirza Gibbs looked awkward. 'Well, no. We exchanged a few words and he drove away.'

Dr Peters shook his head at her. 'Thirza, I suspect that you bit the man's head off. We're all used to you in the village, but a stranger might be taken aback.'

'Perhaps I was a bit sharp. But now we know who he is we can write to him and express our gratitude.' She gave Katrina an enquiring look as she spoke.

Katrina said, with a bit of a snap, 'Aunt Thirza, we agreed that he would have forgotten us.'

'I doubt that,' said Dr Peters, 'seeing that his whole day was disorganised.'

'Well, I think we're making a lot of fuss about nothing. I'll write a letter if you want me to, Aunt, but I doubt if he'll read it—he'll have a secretary to deal with his letters—or his wife,' she added slowly. He would be married, of course, with two children, a comfortable house in a good area of town and probably a country cottage or a villa on the Algarve. Even if she didn't like him, that was no reason to grudge him success in life.

Dr Peters said, 'I think a letter would be civil, don't you? And by the way, he's a professor—I looked him up in my medical directory. Simon Glenville—you could send it to the hospital. He's got consulting rooms but I haven't the address.'

He went presently, and as he and Miss Gibbs

walked to the gate he said, 'Katrina's been a bit shaken; make her go gently for a couple of days. It isn't like her to be snappy.'

Which was true enough, for she was a warm-natured and kind girl, liked by everyone in the village, always ready to give a hand where it was wanted, and, unlike her aunt, prepared to like everyone who crossed her path. All except, for some reason, the man who had come to her aid that morning. But that was no reason to be ungrateful to him. That evening Katrina sat down and composed a polite note to him. It took several attempts to get it right but, pleased with the final result, she posted it the next day and told herself that was the end of the affair.

Of course, she had to make a statement to the police, and then scour Warminster for a second-hand bike; a new one was out of the question and the pity of it was that she hadn't been insured. But there had to be some means of transport. A bus went into Warminster each day, but bus fares were costly and she had long ago taken over the shopping, loading up once a week and going to the village stores for day-to-day needs. And they weren't many, for she and her aunt lived frugally, growing vegetables in the garden behind the cottage, getting eggs from Lovegrove's Farm along the road. It was amazing what a number of meals one could conjure from eggs.

Katrina wondered during the next few days about Professor Glenville; she might not have liked him, but she so seldom left the village that anyone not connected with it was of interest, however slight. But she didn't speak of him to her aunt, and neither did that lady mention him. Her accident had been a small disruption in their quiet life, and neither she nor her aunt were given to dwelling on any mishap they might encounter.

Katrina made light of her bruises and cuts, did the bulk of the household chores, dug the garden and, once she had her new bike, shopped. The event had caused something of a stir in the village, which was so small and out of the way that anything outside its normal gentle routine was a subject for talk for several days. The people living there liked her and were vaguely sorry for her. It was no life for a pretty girl, living in that poky cottage with an elderly aunt, never meeting any young men. Several of them had hinted as much to her face, but she had fobbed them off, saying that she was very happy and had no wish for the bright lights.

'But you'd have money to buy lovely clothes, and meet people,' one well-wisher had reminded her.

'But there are people here,' Katrina had pointed out, 'and when would I wear lovely clothes?' And she had added in a voice which had effectively closed the conversation, 'I'm happy here.'

Which wasn't quite true. She wasn't *un*happy, but she *was* young and pretty and full of life; pretty clothes, visits to the theatre, dining out, dancing—she wished that she could sample them all, while at the same time knowing that it was most unlikely.

She had lived with Aunt Thirza since her parents had been killed in a plane crash when she was twelve years old. She had no brothers or sisters; there were numerous aunts and uncles and cousins, but Aunt Thirza was the only one of the family who had given her a home. That had been twelve years ago, before she had retired as headmistress of a girls' school—a privately run establishment where Katrina had been educated. When Aunt Thirza had retired Katrina had been seventeen, and hopeful of going on to university. But it seemed that that wouldn't be possible. Aunt Thirza had pointed out in her forthright way that she had only her pension, which would not stretch to it.

'But something may turn up,' she had said. 'I suggest that you stay at home with me. You're still young; a year or two won't matter at your age. I shall write to your uncles and aunts and enlist their help. After all, they were your father's brothers and sisters.'

However, offers of help had not been forthcoming. Did Thirza not realise that Katrina's cousins were a constant drain on parental purses? Had she any idea what it cost to give them a start in life?

Vague offers of help in a year or two had been made, and so she had stifled her disappointment and agreed with her aunt that a year or so living at the cottage would be delightful. She had made a tentative offer to find work of some sort; she had her A levels, and she was quick and intelligent—a job in Warminster, perhaps? In a shop or as a dental assistant...

Aunt Thirza had been disapproving. 'No niece of mine will waste her talents in a shop,' she had said vigorously. 'If your cousins can go to university, then so shall you. It is merely a question of waiting for a year or two.'

But the years had slipped by, and the cousins, no longer at university had still been a constant expense to their parents. The girls became engaged, and expected splendid weddings, the young men naturally needed allowances while they found their feet earning their living in something suitable.

After a few years Aunt Thirza had given up talking about university, and Katrina's pleas to get a job had also been swept aside. She had plenty to keep her busy. She had taken over most of the household chores now that Aunt Thirza was getting on a bit, and besides, there was the garden, the Youth Club in the village, the church flowers, the various bazaars and fêtes—regular events. And she had friends, as Aunt Thirza had pointed out. Her aunt had ended by asking her if she wasn't happy, in a voice which shook a little, and Katrina, seeing the unhappiness in the elderly face, had assured her that she was very happy.

And after that she gave up talking about jobs or university; her aunt had given her a home and affection when no one else was willing to do so, and she was deeply grateful for that. Besides, she was fond of the old lady.

Professor Glenville drove himself home, cutting across country along narrow, less used roads to Wherwell, a village tucked away in Hampshire but near enough to the motorway for him to travel to and fro to London each day, where he had consulting rooms as well as beds at St Aldrick's. His friends and colleagues thought him crazy, living away from London, but he found the early-morning drive to his rooms a pleasant start to his day, even in bad weather, and, however late at night, he made a point of returning to Wherwell; only in an emergency would he spend the night at the small flat above his consulting rooms.

As he drove he decided what he would do with the rest of his day. He had been in Bristol for several days, for he was an examiner for several hospitals, but now he was free until the morning—he could do some writing, catch up on his reading, potter in his garden and take the dogs for a walk, and Mrs Peach, who ran his home with Peach, would give him a splendid tea...

He allowed his thoughts to dwell on Miss Thirza Gibbs and her niece, but only briefly, thinking it a pity, though, that Katrina had been so tart. Even making allowances for shock she need not have been quite so frosty. As for her aunt, he had been in his profession long enough to recognise her type—sharp-tongued, never looking for sympathy, and hiding a soft heart beneath a brisk manner. He decided that he rather liked her.

Wherwell was a delightful village, most of its houses thatched, the country around it peaceful. He drove down its main street and turned into a narrow lane, and then through open gates to his home, which was black and white timber-framed with its thatched roof curling round the upstairs windows. It was a fair size, and the garden around it was sheltered by trees. He drove round the side, parked the car, and went in through the side door, along a flagstoned passage and into the kitchen. Peach and his wife were there. She sat at the table rolling out pastry, Peach at the other end of the table, cleaning the silver.

Peach got up at once. 'Good afternoon, sir,' he said mildly. 'You'll be wanting lunch...'

'No, no, Peach. One of Mrs Peach's magnificent teas in half an hour would be fine. Everything all right?'

'Right as rain, sir. Barker and Jones are in the garden. Tea in half an hour, sir.'

The professor picked up his bag and went through a door into the hall, which was long and narrow with a door at each end. He opened his study door, put his bag on the desk and went out of the end door into the garden. Two dogs were waiting for him, uttering pleased barks, running to him as he bent to fondle them: a coal-black Alsatian and a small dog of no known parentage, with a foxy face, heavy whiskers and a feathery tail. The three of them made their way down a path bordered by flowerbeds already full of colour, skirted a large lawn with a small pond at its end and went through a gate into the fields beyond. The dogs raced on ahead now, and the professor sauntered along, his thoughts idle, vaguely irritated that they turned every so often to the events of the other morning.

He went indoors presently, to Mrs Peach's tea, and then spent an hour or so in his study with his dogs for company. He went back there after his dinner too, making notes for the book he was writing concerning his work. He was a clever man, wrapped up in his profession but by no means a hermit; he had friends, close friends he had known for years, and a host of acquaintances and family scattered throughout the country, but as yet he had found no one whom he wished to make his wife. And that was a pity, Peach had confided to his wife. A good man like the master ought to have been married years ago, with a handful of children. 'Knocking forty,' Peach had grumbled. 'And dear knows he meets enough ladies to pick and choose.'

'She'll turn up,' said Mrs Peach. 'Just you let Fate take its course.' Fate must have been listening.

It was a week or so after Katrina's accident that she noticed that Aunt Thirza didn't look well. Indeed, now she thought about it, she hadn't looked well for some weeks. But Aunt Thirza wasn't a woman to angle for sympathy for herself, and when once or twice Katrina had asked her if she felt all right, she had responded in her usual blunt manner. All the same, there was no denying that she was paler than usual, and lacked energy. And when one morning Katrina found her sitting in the living room with her eyes shut, instead of turning out the sideboard drawers which she had intended to do, Katrina took matters into her own hands.

Despite her aunt's protests, she got on her bike and went to Dr Peters' surgery and left a message with his receptionist. It wasn't a day on which the surgery was open, but she knew that he would come and see her aunt as soon as he could; they had been friends for years and, however brusque Aunt Thirza was feeling, she would listen to his advice.

He came that evening, examined his old friend, taking no notice of her waspish replies to his questions and, despite her protests, taking a sample of her blood.

'Well, what's wrong with me?' demanded Aunt Thirza.

'You've been doing too much,' he told her, and Katrina thought that she detected the impersonal cheerfulness with which the medical profession conceal their true opinion. 'I'll get this blood tested—it will take a day or two. I'll let you know when I've the result and give you something to put you back on your feet. In the meantime, just take things easily. You won't, of course!'

Three days later he called again. 'Anaemia,' he told her. 'Nothing which can't be put right with treatment. But I want you to see a specialist, just to endorse my opinion.' And when Miss Gibbs began an indignant refusal, he said, 'No, Thirza, my dear. We want the quickest solution, don't we? So we'll get expert advice.'

Katrina, walking with him to the gate, said, 'Is it serious, Dr Peters?'

'Perhaps, my dear. We must see what the specialist says. I'll get an appointment for your aunt. You'll go with her, of course.'

When he got back to his surgery he lifted the phone and asked to speak to Professor Glenville.

# CHAPTER TWO

AUNT THIRZA was surprised to receive a letter within the next few days, bidding her to attend a clinic at St Aldrick's on the following Monday. She was inclined to grumble about this—such short notice and the awkward journey to the hospital. 'A waste of time,' she declared. 'I think I shall not go.'

Katrina waited for her first annoyance to subside before saying mildly, 'Well, since Dr Peters had taken the trouble to arrange for someone to see you it would be rather unkind to refuse to go. The appointment's for eleven o'clock—we can catch an early train from Warminster and probably be home again by teatime.'

Bob from the garage drove them to the station—an unavoidable extravagance which for once Miss Gibbs ignored. It was a lovely morning, warm for the time of year, so that Katrina was able to wear the jersey dress and matching jacket which she kept for special occasions. And this *was* a special occasion—a day out in London, even if most of it would be spent on a bench in the hospital waiting room. The unbidden thought that she might see Professor Glenville again she squashed instantly; he would have forgotten about her, and even if he hadn't he would hardly wish to renew their acquaintance...

The waiting room was large and crowded, and although they were in good time a nurse told them that they would probably have to wait for half an hour or so.

Aunt Thirza was tired, and had no objection to sitting quietly, and Katrina found plenty to interest her. Moreover, there was always the chance that Professor Glenville might appear. Unlikely, she thought. She didn't know much about hospitals, but she thought that a well-known man such as Dr Peters had described would have consulting rooms, and only go to the hospital for some emergency or consultation.

It was almost noon by the time Miss Gibbs' name was called.

'I prefer to go by myself, Katrina,' she said firmly. 'No doubt if you are needed someone will come and tell you.'

She went off with a nurse, her back as stiff as a poker, and was ushered into one of the consulting rooms where she was asked to sit down while a sister took her blood pressure, her temperature, and asked her if she took medicine of any sort, and, if so, what?

'I do not believe in pills and potions,' said Aunt Thirza severely. 'I am a healthy woman and do not need such things.'

Sister murmured in a non-committal manner and ushered her into the inner room, going to stand by the desk facing the door. Miss Gibbs fetched up by it. 'Oh, it's you!' she declared sharply. 'I do hope you understand that I have only agreed to come because Dr Peters and I are old friends and I wished to oblige him.'

The professor stood up and offered a hand. 'Miss Gibbs. This is tiresome for you, I feel sure. Please sit down and tell me how I can help you.'

Miss Gibbs sat, still very erect. 'I owe you an apology, Professor. I was much at fault not to express my gratitude for your help.'

'Most understandable in the circumstances, Miss Gibbs.' He had become politely remote. 'And now, if you would answer a few questions? This shouldn't take long.'

Aunt Thirza gave succinct replies to his quiet questions, watching him write them down. He looked very reassuring sitting there, and very handsome, too, and his manner was calming, although she told herself that she had no reason to be alarmed. He looked up presently.

'If you would go with Sister, she will help you to undress. I shall need to examine you.'

'Is that really necessary?'

'Yes, Miss Gibbs.' He glanced at Sister, who whisked Aunt Thirza into another small room, peeled her clothes off her with a practised hand, wrapped her in a shapeless white garment and helped her onto the couch. And when the professor came she took possession of an elderly hand and gave it a reassuring squeeze so that Aunt Thirza, with nothing more than an annoyed snort, relaxed under his gentle hands.

Presently, once more dressed, her sensible hat firmly on her head again, she sat facing him at his desk. 'Well,' she asked, 'are you going to tell me what is wrong? If there is anything wrong...'

'You have anaemia, Miss Gibbs, something which we can deal with. I shall write to Dr Peters with my suggestions for your treatment and I should like to see you again. Shall we say in two weeks' time?'

'If you think it is necessary,' Aunt Thirza said grumpily. 'It is quite a long journey.'

He said smoothly, 'You have someone with you today? Your niece?'

'Katrina, yes.' She gave him a sharp look, but he only smiled blandly.

'I'm sorry I have no time in which to meet her again. Please thank her for her letter.'

The letter, so stiff and written with obvious reluctance, had made him smile.

He stood up and shook hands, and when Sister came back from ushering Aunt Thirza out, he said, 'A pity. It's lymphatic leukaemia, and I suspect she has had it for some time. We'll treat it, of course. There is always a chance that she will live for a number of years. Luckily it isn't rapid. But it is fatal...'

'A nice old thing, too,' said Sister. 'There's a very pretty girl with her.'

'That will be her niece.' He made a mental note to talk to Katrina and explain about her aunt. Miss Gibbs was a strong-minded old lady, but he had no intention of telling her the truth until necessary.

He sat writing at his desk and found himself wondering what would happen to Katrina if Miss Gibbs were to die. He wished he had seen her again. The temptation had been great to send a nurse with a message asking her to see him, but then Aunt Thirza would have smelled a rat. He must arrange to go to Dr Peters' surgery so that he could explain about her aunt's illness.

He asked for his next patient and forgot Katrina.

But he remembered again as he drove himself home that evening. Katrina would have to be told the true state of affairs—something which Dr Peters was quite able to do, but which for some reason he felt obliged to do himself.

Life, for the next few days, returned to normal for Aunt Thirza and Katrina. Dr Peters came, prescribed pills, advised rest, no excitement and a suitable diet, offered reassurance and went away again, with the suggestion that Katrina should collect the pills the next morning at the surgery.

'Such a fuss,' said Aunt Thirza, but for once did what she had been told to do, sitting down with her knitting and allowing Katrina to get on with the household chores.

While she hung out the washing and pulled radishes and lettuce for their lunch Katrina allowed her faint suspicions to surface. Dr Peters had been almost too reassuring. She would ask him to tell her exactly what was wrong in the morning...

There was no need, for when she went into the surgery he told her. 'We do not need to give up hope,' he said. 'Your aunt's illness is almost always slow in its progress, and she is elderly.' He glanced at her to see if she had understood and she nodded. 'There is no reason to tell her at the moment, but if at any time she should ask then Professor Glenville will explain it to her. By the way, he is coming here on Sunday; he thinks it advisable that he should talk to you so that you understand fully and know what to expect.'

She said rather tartly, 'Is there any need for that? Surely you can tell me anything I need to know.'

Dr Peters said mildly, 'My dear, Professor Glenville is at the very top of his profession. If there is a way by which your aunt can be helped he will do that, but he would need co-operation, and you are the one to give that. He suggests that I invite your aunt to spend Sunday with us. She and Mary are old friends; there is plenty for them to gossip about. And when she is safely out of the house the professor will call on you.'

'He won't expect lunch?'

Dr Peters hid a smile. 'Most unlikely! A cup of coffee should suffice. You don't like him, Katrina?'

'I'm not sure...'

'But you trust him?'

'Yes, and I'll do anything to help Aunt Thirza.' She hesitated. 'I suppose you don't know how long?'

'No, my dear, I don't. That is a question for Professor Glenville; he will be better able to answer than I.'

So Katrina went back home with a note from Mrs Peters, and Aunt Thirza agreed with pleasure to spend the day with her friends. 'You won't be lonely, Katrina? I know it wouldn't be very interesting for you to accompany me, but it might be preferable to sitting here on your own.'

'I shan't sit,' said Katrina promptly. 'There's heaps of work in the garden, and I can get on with it without being interrupted. I've all those lettuces to transplant, and the rhubarb to pull, and I want to dig that empty patch at the bottom of the garden. Remember those seedlings I got from the farm? If I don't get them in there won't be any peas later on.'

Dr Peters was coming for her aunt soon after ten o'clock on Sunday, so Katrina was up early, tidying the little house, getting breakfast, and making sure that her aunt had all she needed for her day out. As she herself was going to work in the garden she had got into an elderly cotton jersey dress, faded to a gentle blue and, had she but known it, very flattering to her shapely curves. She had no intention of dressing up just because Professor Glenville chose to call. She tied her hair back with a ribbon and dug her feet into sandals. Digging was hot work, and now that it was May the days were warmer.

Her aunt safely away, Katrina put the coffee pot on the stove, cups and saucers on a tray with a tin of biscuits, and went down the garden to the shed at the bottom. She found her fork and spade, a trug for the rhubarb, and set to work. First the rhubarb...

She had the trug half full when the professor drew up silently, opened the gate, mindful of its creaking, and trod up the path to the open door of the house. There was no answer to his knock, naturally enough, and after a few moments he wandered down the garden to be rewarded by the sight of Katrina, bent double over the rhubarb.

His quiet, 'Good morning, Katrina,' brought her upright, clutching an armful of pink stalks.

'Oh, Lord...I didn't expect you so soon.'

He kept a straight face. 'Shall I go for a drive around while you finish your gardening?'

'I'm not gardening, only pulling rhubarb. I was going to dig that patch over there.' She pointed with a stick of the fruit. 'I told Aunt Thirza I would and she'll wonder why if it isn't done.'

'The pair of us should be able to get that done later on...'

At her look of surprise, he added, 'I like gardening.'

'You do? All right. I don't suppose it will take long, whatever it is that you have to tell me.' She dusted off her grubby hands. 'Come and have a cup of coffee first.' She added belatedly, 'This must be spoiling your Sunday?'

The professor, beginning to enjoy himself, assured her that it was still early and he had the whole day before him.

'I expect you are glad to be out of London for the day,' said Katrina, leading the way into the house.

They had their coffee in the little living room, with the sun shining in on the rather shabby chairs and the polished sofa table and old-fashioned chiffonnier, both old and valuable. It shone on Katrina's wealth of hair, too, and the professor admired it silently. A strikingly lovely girl, he had to admit, who made no effort to engage his attention.

When she had refilled their cups, Katrina said, 'What was it you wanted to tell me? It's about Aunt Thirza, of course. Dr Peters said he would prefer you to explain in more detail.' For a moment she faltered.

'Your aunt has lymphatic leukaemia, which is incurable, although there is a great deal to be done which can prolong her life. But one must consider the fact that she is no longer young. It is a slow-moving illness. Indeed it can be compatible with a normal lifespan.'

Katrina didn't look at him; she was staring out of the window. 'You mean that Aunt Thirza might— might live until her death without knowing?'

'Yes, that is exactly what I do mean. Unless she asks me to tell her chapter and verse, in which case I should do so. I hope that will not happen, and I suggest that she is allowed to believe that she has a simple anaemia which we shall treat in the prescribed way. She is a sensible lady, is she not? And she will go along with any treatment we suggest—pills, of course, diet, rest.' He added abruptly, 'You can cope with that?'

'Yes, of course I can.' She looked at him then, and he saw that her eyes were filled with tears. 'I owe everything to Aunt Thirza. She gave me a home when no one else wanted me.'

A tear escaped and trickled down her cheek, and for a moment he had a vision of a small sad girl whom no one had wanted. He offered a beautifully laundered handkerchief and said nothing; he sensed that if he did speak she would dislike him even more. He had been the bearer of bad news, and now he had seen her in tears. He sat quietly until she had mopped her face and mumbled that she would launder his handkerchief and send it to him.

'I never cry,' she told him fiercely.

'How old were you when you came to live here?' He sounded friendly, and she responded to the sound of his quiet voice.

'Twelve. Mother and Father died in an air crash on their way back from the Middle East. Father built bridges and sometimes Mother went with him.'

'No brothers or sisters? No family other than your aunt?'

'No, but several other aunts and uncles, and cousins...' She broke off. 'This is boring for you. Will you tell me what you intend to do for Aunt Thirza and advise me as to the best way to look after her?'

'Certainly I will.' He glanced out of the window. 'It's a lovely morning. Would you come back with me to my home and have lunch? We can discuss every small detail at our leisure.'

'Lunch?' said Katrina. 'Lunch with you?' Her unflattering surprise caused his thin mouth to twitch with sudden amusement. 'But I can't; I've got that digging to do.' She added belatedly, 'Thank you.'

Over the years the professor had cultivated a bed-side manner second to none: courteous and matter-of-fact, nicely laced with sympathy.

'How would it be if I do the digging while you do whatever you need to do? Don't dress up; it will only be the two of us.'

Just as though he couldn't care less what I look like, thought Katrina peevishly. She said loudly, 'You can't dig in those clothes...'

He wore beautifully cut trousers, an open-necked shirt and a cashmere sweater, not to mention the shoes on his large feet.

He didn't answer her but got to his feet. 'Fifteen minutes be long enough?' he wanted to know, and went unhurriedly into the garden.

'The nerve of him,' said Katrina to herself, clashing cups and saucers together, and then spun round.

'Nerve is something which the medical profession have to employ from time to time, Katrina. You don't mind if I call you Katrina?' he said mildly. 'You don't look like a Miss Gibbs. I came back to ask if there is a bigger spade?'

'In the shed.'

He went away again, and she put everything in the sink and went up to her room. She wasn't going to change her dress, for it was apparent to her that he couldn't care less what she wore, but she changed her old sandals for a better pair and attacked her mane of hair, subduing it to tidiness and a neat coil in the nape of her neck. She powdered her face too, and used lipstick, took a quick look at herself in the

little mirror on the dressing table and went downstairs.

She was spooning cat food into a bowl for the little
cat when the professor joined her. He noted the lipstick, and the tidy head of hair, but all he said was,
'What is your cat's name?'

'Betsy.'

She put the saucer on the floor for the small creature and said, 'Had I better come and look?'

He had made a very good job of it. Moreover he
had managed to remain as elegant as he had been
when he arrived. She thanked him warmly, forgetting
how much he vexed her for the moment, and when
he asked her if she was ready to leave said that she
was, quite meekly. 'Only I must just open the window in the kitchen so that Betsy can get in and out.'

They went out together, and he locked the door
and put the key above it out of sight. 'At what time
shall your aunt return?'

'She is to spend the day with the Peterses, so soon
after tea, I suppose. Supposing she comes back earlier and I am not here?'

'We will worry about that when it happens.'

Getting into the car, she asked, 'Where do you
live? In London? We'll never get there and back...'

'I live in Wherwell—a village south of Andover.
I go to and fro to town; it's an easy drive.'

It was a matter of thirty-five miles or so, and the
big car swallowed them effortlessly. Beyond a casual
remark from time to time the professor didn't speak,
and Katrina was glad of that as she tried to look into
the future.

Of course she had always known that Aunt Thirza
wouldn't live for ever, but she had dismissed such

thoughts from her mind as morbid. Her aunt had always seemed the same to her: brisk and matter-of-fact, full of energy, with a finger in every village pie. And as to her own future she had taught herself not to dwell too much on that. She was twenty-four, and the years she might have spent at university and later in some worthwhile job had slipped away, just as her chances of meeting a man who would want to marry her were slipping away.

Indeed, she knew very few young men, and they were either on the verge of marriage or already married. There had been men who had shown an interest in her, of course, but Aunt Thirza had frightened them off, though not intentionally.

She was roused from her thoughts by the professor observing that Wherwell was round the next bend in the country road, and she looked around her.

She fell in love with it immediately. There was no one around and the place drowsed in Sunday calm, the charming houses lining the street grouped round the church like a chocolate box picture.

When he stopped outside his own front door she got out slowly and stood looking around her.

'You live here?' she asked, and blushed because it was such a silly question. 'Such a beautiful house. You're married, of course, and have children?'

He didn't speak for a moment, looking down his splendid nose at her, and the blush, which had been fading, returned with a vengeance.

'I am not married, nor do I have children. There is, of course, always that possibility in the future.'

'I'm sorry. I shouldn't have asked you that. It's none of my business.'

'No. It isn't. You feel that the house is wasted on me?'

'No, no. It's so beautiful—and the garden…'

'Yes. I enjoy the garden; the house has been in the family for a long time.'

Peach had opened the door, gravely welcoming his master and then, when he was introduced to Katrina, shaking the hand she offered. A nice young lady, he thought, a sight nicer than that Mrs Carew. Widow she might be, and handsome enough, but never so much as wished him good day. If ever she managed to marry the professor Peach felt in his bones that he and Mrs Peach would be in for a rough time.

He said now, 'The dogs are in the garden, sir.' And indeed their barks made that evident enough. 'Would you and Miss Gibbs like coffee?'

'No, thanks, Peach, we've had it. May we have lunch in half an hour or so? We have to go back in a couple of hours.'

'I'll tell Mrs Peach. Would the young lady like to refresh herself?'

The professor eyed Katrina. 'She looks all right to me.'

He lifted eyebrows at Katrina, who said coldly, 'Thank you, not at the moment.'

'Good. We'll be in the garden, Peach.'

He walked her down the hall and out of the door at its end, to be met by Barker and Jones. Katrina offered a fist to Barker. 'He's beautiful,' she said, and scratched the top of his sleek head, and then bent down to do the same for Jones.

'Why Jones?' she asked.

'We are not quite sure, but we suspect that there may be Welsh blood in him. A trace of Corgi.'

'They're friends?'

'Oh, yes. Jones is Barker's faithful follower!'

He led the way along a garden path to a gazebo overlooking a pool fed by a small rivulet emerging from a clump of trees at the end of the garden. Katrina sat down and looked about her. The garden wasn't formal; it was like a large cottage garden. In full summer, she supposed, it would be full of old-fashioned flowers. One side sloped downhill to the kitchen garden, with high walls, thatched like the house, and on the other side there was a wide green path bordered by flowerbeds. She gave a sigh of content.

'Will you tell me what I must do to help Aunt Thirza? And what sort of treatment she is to have.'

'That is my intention. Bad news is never as bad if it is given in the right surroundings, is it? Now sit still and don't interrupt...'

He didn't try to make light of the matter, but neither was he full of gloomy forebodings. 'We must take each day as it comes. Your aunt may fail so slowly that it is barely noticeable; on the other hand she may die without any warning. If you can accept that, it will help you. Don't stop her from doing what she wishes to do. I think that she is someone who would dislike being an invalid, but try and discreetly curb her activities as much as possible. Dr Peters will be keeping an eye on her and will keep you up to date. Now, as to diet...'

Katrina listened carefully, and the thought crossed her mind that perhaps she didn't dislike him after all. She didn't *like* him, but only because she knew nothing about him, and she *was* grateful to him...

The professor glanced at his watch, whistled the

dogs, and they went back to the house to have lunch.
Aunt Thirza wasn't mentioned again. Instead he led
the talk to Katrina's own interests, slipping in questions about her life so that by the time they left the
table he had a very good idea of it. And pretty dull
too, he reflected, watching her pour coffee into the
delicate porcelain coffee cups. She might be buried
alive in the country, but she had the potential for a
career of some sort. He asked abruptly, 'How old are
you, Katrina?'

'Twenty-four. Don't you know it's rude to ask a
girl how old she is?'

'I stand corrected. Unfortunately it is a question I
have to ask all my patients—it has become a bad
habit.'

'Oh, well, I don't mind. How old are you,
Professor?'

He laughed, and she thought that he looked ten
years younger. 'Thirty-nine. Middle-aged.'

'Rubbish, no one is middle-aged these days. You
were fifteen when I was born...'

'You had a happy childhood, Katrina, for those
first twelve years?'

She nodded. 'Yes.' She wanted to ask him if he
had been happy as a boy, but she didn't dare. She
mustn't allow herself to get too friendly with him,
although she didn't think that there was much fear
of that. He would never allow it.

Presently he said, 'We should be going,' and she
got to her feet at once, anxious not to outstay her
welcome.

'It was kind of you to ask me to come here,' she
told him. 'I hope I haven't spoilt your day.' And,
when Peach came into the hall, she said, 'Will you

tell Mrs Peach that lunch was lovely? I wish I could cook like that.'

Indeed it had been lovely. Potted shrimps and brown bread and butter, cut wafer-thin, rack of lamb with tiny new potatoes, and rhubarb fool to follow with clotted cream. The professor certainly lived well. Sitting beside him in the car, she wondered if he earned a great deal of money, and thought he probably did. Dr Peters had said that he was highly regarded, and of course it must cost a great deal to train as a doctor. She voiced her thoughts out loud.

'Does it cost a lot of money to train as a doctor?'

If he was surprised by her question he didn't show it. 'Yes, but it isn't only the money; it's the years of hard work.'

'Have you been a doctor for a long time?'

'I qualified when I was twenty-three…'

'But you took more exams, I expect?'

'Any number.'

'But you've got there, haven't you? I mean, to the top of your particular tree?'

'Perhaps, but there is always something more to learn.' He glanced at her. 'Have you ever wished to train for a profession, Katrina?'

'Oh, yes. You know how it is when you leave school; you're full of ideas. But I'm happy with Aunt Thirza, and I'd hate to live in a town—a big town.'

He drew up outside the cottage, got out and opened her door. The little house looked charming in the afternoon sun, and Betsy was sitting by the door, waiting for them. He took the key from its hiding place, unlocked the door and they all went in.

Katrina let out a breath. 'How awful if Aunt Thirza had been here. Whatever would I have told her?'

'Oh, I would have thought of something feasible before you had a chance to blurt out the truth. Shall we have tea?'

'Is there time?' She was putting the kettle on the gas ring as she spoke. She suddenly didn't want to be left alone with her thoughts.

They drank their tea presently, not saying much and not mentioning Aunt Thirza either, and soon the professor got into his car and drove away. Katrina had thanked him for her lunch, for digging the garden, for his advice, and he had put up a large hand and begged her to say no more, so that she had the lowering feeling that she had been too effusive.

But she had other things to think about. While she got the supper ready she went over everything that the professor had told her; she mustn't forget a word of it...

Aunt Thirza returned, full of good spirits, and Dr Peters stayed for a while, chatting about their day. 'We must do it more often,' he observed. 'You and Mary have much in common, and she's absolutely delighted that you've agreed to help with the church bazaar.' He glanced at Katrina. 'I suppose you'll be expected to give a hand, Katrina?'

'I'm behind the scenes this year, cutting sandwiches and serving teas.'

Over supper Aunt Thirza was full of plans. 'I do so enjoy the summer months,' she explained. 'Such a lot going on—fêtes and bazaars and tennis tournaments, and I hear that the church school is putting on a play at the end of term. More than enough to keep us busy.'

She put down her knife and fork. 'I had such a

splendid lunch I'm really not hungry. Did you get the digging done?'

Katrina said that yes, she had. Well, it wasn't quite a fib put that way. 'There's still a lot to do. Everything's growing nicely, though. We need some rain.'

It was surprising how difficult it was to talk about mundane things when what she really wanted to do was to fling her arms round her aunt and have a good howl.

The days slipped away in the orderly routine which Aunt Thirza had established when she retired and had no intention of altering. Katrina did her best to check the old lady's more active interests, but it wasn't easy. Indeed, Aunt Thirza had remarked once or twice that anyone would think that she was ill.

'Those pills I take will soon put me back on my feet,' she observed. 'There are any number of things which I wish to do this summer.'

Since there was no gainsaying her, Katrina gave up urging her to eat the tasty meals she cooked, and drink the milk Dr Peters had told her would improve her condition, although she managed in a dozen ways to take over more of the household chores, pointing out that her aunt was busy enough with the various functions being organised.

But Aunt Thirza wasn't getting better. Katrina could see that she was paler and easily tired, although she would never admit it, and Dr Peters had told her that her latest blood test showed no improvement.

'But it's not worse?'

He said cautiously, 'Let us say that it is no better.' Which to Katrina's ears didn't sound like an answer at all.

They were to go to St Aldrick's very shortly. Aunt Thirza had had a letter from the professor's secretary, asking her to attend his clinic.

'You'll come with me,' said Aunt Thirza, 'and if he doesn't keep me hanging around for too long we will have a look at the shops. I need some new tea-towels—John Lewis will do nicely.'

It was already warm by the time they set out, and when they reached the hospital Aunt Thirza was tired and ill tempered.

'This is nonsense,' she told Katrina. 'I'm sure there is no need for Professor Glenville to see me again. I feel perfectly well except for this tiredness, and that's to be expected when you are as old as I am.'

'You're only seventy-something,' Katrina reminded her. 'I dare say this will be the last time, just to check that everything is going according to plan.'

She sat quietly and wondered if she would see the professor. It seemed unlikely, for it wasn't a social call and there were rows of patients for him to see. Her aunt was one of many, and she wondered again just how eminent he was. What did he do in his free time? He had hinted that he might marry, so he would spend his evenings with whoever it was he intended to marry. Did they go dancing, she wondered, or dine at some marvellous restaurant? Or did she go home with him and spend the evening eating Mrs Peach's delicious dinners?

A nurse called her aunt's name and Katrina watched her disappear down the short corridor lined with doors. The professor's room was the nearest. She glanced at her watch. They had been waiting for more than half an hour and her aunt would be fifteen minutes or so. If they were to go to the shops they would have to catch a later train.

Aunt Thirza came back, some twenty minutes later, her back poker-straight, looking annoyed. She marched out with Katrina hurrying to keep up with her.

Outside, on the pavement of the busy street, Katrina said, 'What has he told you, Aunt, something to upset you?'

Her heart gave a sickening thump. Surely her aunt hadn't asked an outright question, demanded the truth?

'He says I must come here again in three weeks' time. It seems the anaemia isn't responding to treatment. It sometimes happens, he told me, and I must have patience. It may take a little longer than he had hoped. I have to get more pills from Dr Peters.' She smiled suddenly. 'Last time I was here we mentioned the garden, and he said he had noticed that there was a small moss rose under the window, not doing too well. He has to come our way on Sunday and he asked if I would accept a rose bush—he has several in his garden and will need to discard a few. He'll come for coffee.'

'How kind,' said Katrina, wondering just why he was doing that, and planning to bake a batch of her almond biscuits which sold so well at village functions. The news wasn't good, but hopefully she would get the chance to ask him what exactly was happening. Surely there was something, some treatment—a blood transfusion—to halt her aunt's illness.

'Well, don't look so glum,' said Aunt Thirza, once more her brisk self. 'He's rather nice. Now, let's get a bus to Oxford Street.'

# CHAPTER THREE

THE teatowels were bought, and furnished a splendid excuse to roam around John Lewis, looking at the latest goods on show.

'What a good thing that we live in the country and don't need to dress up,' said Aunt Thirza, leading the way to the restaurant. And Katrina, with a last lingering look at the pretty clothes she was never likely to possess, followed her. They didn't mention the professor over their sandwiches and coffee, and Katrina, seeing her aunt's tired face, declared that she had a splitting headache and would Aunt Thirza mind awfully if they caught the earlier train home?

On Sunday morning Katrina got up early to make the almond biscuits, set a tray with the best china and the silver spoons, fed Betsy, and then took a cup of tea to her aunt. Her suggestion that her aunt might like her breakfast in bed called forth a snappy response. Breakfast in bed was only for those too lazy to get up, who should be ashamed of themselves, or in case of necessity—illness, or a broken leg or something similar. 'And I'm not hungry—just tea and toast. I'll be down in half an hour.'

They would be unable to go to morning church; they would go to Evensong instead, which meant that Katrina had the day in which to do a few odd jobs in the garden. That would mean doing the wash on Monday, she reflected, bundling up her hair, and going in to Warminster on Tuesday, since her aunt had observed that now that it was rather warm during the day she found the journey by bus rather tedious. So Katrina had offered to do the shopping in her stead, and had been told sharply that she might do it for this once.

'Next week I shall feel more like it, and it may be cooler,' Miss Gibbs had said. 'Besides, I have a rather busy week ahead of me—there's the parish council meeting, and Mary Peters wants me to help her plan the summer fête.'

Professor Glenville arrived shortly after ten o'clock. As he walked up the garden path Miss Gibbs came to the door.

'Good morning, Professor, and isn't it a splendid one? I hope you haven't come out of your way to bring the rose? You'll stay for a few minutes and have coffee?'

'Yes, thank you. You look very well today.'

'Oh, I feel splendid. The treatment must be working at last. There's so much to be done I'm thankful for that.'

They had gone to sit down on the garden bench. 'Nothing too strenuous, I hope?'

'No, no—but I am on several committees in the village...'

Delighted to find a listener to her rather autocratic views on village life, Miss Gibbs talked happily until Katrina came with the coffee tray.

The professor wished her good morning, got up and fetched the rickety table on which to put the tray, and sat down again, very much at ease. He drank his coffee, ate most of the biscuits and then asked if he might have a spade.

'The rose is in the boot. I'll fetch it and plant it

for you,' he told Miss Gibbs. 'Where would you like it?'

They settled on the sunny wall of the house, facing south and sheltered from cold winds, and he went off to fetch the rose.

'I'll find a spade,' said Katrina, and took a long time about it so that he came down to the shed. 'Do you want to tell me something?' she asked.

'Yes. Not good news, I'm afraid, but I think you must be told. The last blood tests have confirmed my findings when your aunt came to see me. She is going downhill very fast and I must warn you that she may die at any moment.'

Katrina sat down on an upturned box. 'I see.' She had gone rather white but her voice held only the faintest quiver. 'Thank you for warning me. Are you sure? Is there no chance of improvement?'

'No. I'm sorry, and I'm not going to pretend to you that there is. This is the wrong time to tell you, but you're not on the phone, and in any case it isn't something one telephones about. Is there anything I can do to help in any way?'

'No, thank you, you've been very kind. I—I hope that Aunt Thirza dies in her sleep.' She got off the box. 'We had better plant the rose. She's happy about that, isn't she?'

'Yes.' He gave her a searching look. 'You're all right? Not going to cry?'

'I can cry later,' said Katrina soberly.

They planted the rose, with Aunt Thirza watching with a sharp eye, giving orders and changing her mind every few minutes. And when it was done she gave it her entire approval.

'How very kind of you to give me a bush which

is already in flower.' She added, with some of her old briskness, 'It's the wrong time of the year, of course. It should have been planted in the autumn...'

'We'll take a chance,' said the professor cheerfully. 'If it doesn't thrive, I'll bring you another one in the autumn.'

He said he must be going, took the spade back to the shed, and Aunt Thirza thanked him with unwonted warmth. 'I suppose you're going to spend the day with friends?'

He said smoothly, 'Indeed I am. It is good to get away from London, even for a few hours. I live in the country, but I spend my days there, and, as you know, St Aldrick's isn't in the best part of town.'

He went unhurriedly, reminding Aunt Thirza that she would be coming to see him again in a few weeks' time, and Katrina, listening to his quiet voice, wondered how he could conceal his knowledge so successfully.

He shook Miss Gibbs' hand, nodded casually at Katrina and drove off, leaving Aunt Thirza to discuss his visit at some length.

'I daresay he has a girlfriend or a fiancée. He's not a young man and he should have a wife and children. I shall ask him when I see him next.'

Katrina said carefully, 'Well, he did mention vaguely that he might be marrying shortly, so I dare say he's engaged.'

'He would have done very nicely for you,' said Aunt Thirza.

'Aunt—he doesn't even like me. I mean, we get on when we meet, but he's not in the least interested in me.'

She collected up the coffee cups and went to see

about lunch. At least he had liked the almond biscuits.

Mrs Peters came for Aunt Thirza the next morning; the doctor's house was at the other end of the village, ten minutes' walk away, and Aunt Thirza had stoutly maintained that she enjoyed a quiet stroll. But Mrs Peters had an excuse ready—collecting some old curtains Katrina had looked out for the village fête—and bore the old lady off, leaving Katrina to get the washing done and hanging on the line before she was brought back at lunchtime.

She had had a most enjoyable morning, she told Katrina, presiding over one of the committee meetings she chaired—and had done for years—but she didn't eat her lunch and went very willingly enough to rest until teatime.

Katrina, making out the shopping list for the next day, wondered if she dared leave her aunt alone. But they needed groceries, and to get her aunt's pension from the bank. There was her state pension to collect from Mrs Dyer's village store and post office too.

Katrina, doing sums, tried to work out ways of being more economical. There was the journey to St Aldrick's too, in a few weeks' time—a quite costly undertaking. Surely the professor could arrange for her aunt to be seen by someone at Warminster Hospital? Probably he hadn't realised that they hadn't much money. Aunt Thirza had always been one to keep up appearances, even though it meant the small economies no one knew about.

She need not have worried about the shopping; the vicar, an elderly man and a great friend of the doctor, called in the morning, accepted coffee, and suggested that if Katrina wanted to go shopping, or whatever, he would be glad to have a chat with her aunt.

'There are still so many things to settle for the bazaar,' he pointed out.

'I do need to go to Warminster,' said Katrina.

'Then go, my dear. I dare say we shall still be deep in plans by the time you get back.'

She accepted with gratitude, cycled into Warminster and came back laden with groceries; there was time to go to Mrs Dyer's too, and get the pension money. Mrs Dyer was a chatty soul, purveyor and receiver of any news and rumours of a local nature.

'How's Miss Gibbs?' she wanted to know. 'Hasn't been looking too spry these last few weeks. I was over at the butcher's and Mr Tapp, he said the same. Seen the doctor, has she?'

Katrina asked for stamps and counted her change. 'Oh, yes. Dr Peters takes good care of her, you know. She finds this warmer weather trying, but she enjoys her committees.'

'Glad of that. She's been our main prop and stay for the village social life for dear knows how long. Wait a sec...' The good soul disappeared into the room behind the shop and came back with a brown paper bag. 'My hens are laying a treat, and I dare say your aunt might like an egg with her tea. There's nothing like a nice new-laid egg.'

'Mrs Dyer, how kind of you. I'm sure she'll enjoy one.'

Mrs Dyer nodded cheerfully, and wondered why Miss Katrina should look so sad.

Her aunt was full of plans for the bazaar; the vicar had suggested dates, and asked her to contact the ladies who usually helped each year and get things organised. Katrina's spirits lifted at the sight of her aunt's enthusiasm. Aunt Thirza appeared to be almost her old self again.

Even clever consultants can make mistakes, reflected Katrina, cutting wafer-thin bread and butter to go with the egg.

Two days later, Aunt Thirza died. They had been in the garden, she and Katrina, sitting on the bench, admiring the moss rose. It was a pleasantly warm afternoon and they hadn't talked much, just sat there, content with each other's company.

Katrina had looked up when her aunt had spoken. 'You've been a good girl, Katrina, I couldn't have wished for a more loving daughter of my own.' She had smiled a little, sighed gently, and died.

Katrina hadn't believed it for a few moments. The professor had warned her, but in her heart of hearts she had believed him to be over-cautious; her aunt had seemed so much better during the last few days. Hard on that thought came a deep thankfulness that Aunt Thirza had died as she would have wished: without fuss and at peace, sitting in her loved garden.

Katrina pulled herself together then, kissed her aunt, murmured a prayer and said, in a voice which didn't sound quite like her own, 'I must leave you, Aunt, while I go and phone. But you're not alone here; the moss rose will keep you company.'

She fetched her bike then, and went to the farm and rang Dr Peters and the vicar, and then went back to her aunt. Aunt Thirza looked as though she was asleep, and it was only then that Katrina began to cry.

She wiped her tears away when Dr Peters came,

followed by the vicar. They carried Aunt Thirza up to her room, and shortly afterwards Mrs Tripp, the local nurse, arrived. The rest of that day didn't seem real, though everyone was so kind. Mrs Peters came and sat quietly while Katrina talked away her first shock and sorrow.

'You must come back and spend the night with us,' she told Katrina kindly.

But Katrina wouldn't do that. 'I shall be quite all right,' she declared. 'I'd rather stay…'

Mrs Peters understood, sat over her while she ate some supper and then went home. Strangely enough, Katrina slept soundly, but her last waking thought was regret that the professor hadn't been there. So silly, she told herself, half-asleep, for what could he have done? Nothing—and everything—for he would have told her to be thankful that Aunt Thirza had had a perfect end to her life. And he would have let her howl her eyes out, told her to pull herself together and offered his handkerchief. She smiled a bit, and snivelled a bit, and slept.

The village, shocked and sympathetic, rallied round. All the same Katrina found that she had so much to do that she had to bury her grief for the time being. Aunt Thirza had brothers and sisters still living—those same brothers and sisters who had found an excuse for not giving Katrina a home and helping with her education, who, in fact, had ignored her. It was years since she had seen them, for they had never come to see Aunt Thirza, although they were punctilious about sending cards at Christmas and on her birthday. All the same, they had to be told of Aunt Thirza's death and be invited to her funeral.

Katrina hadn't expected them to come. What

would be the point? They had ignored the old lady while she was alive. But they came, driving up in their BMWs and Mercedeses, the two aunts pecking Katrina's cheek, the uncles shaking hands and muttering condolences and the cousins, five of them, looking her up and down and barely speaking.

Katrina was polite to them, because that would have pleased Aunt Thirza, who deplored bad manners, but since everyone who possibly could had come from the village the church was full, and she needed only to spend a short time with them. Afterwards they came back to Rose Cottage with her.

'After all, Thirza was our sister,' said the elder of the aunts. 'I dare say she has left us some small memento, and your solicitor will be reading the will, I suppose?'

Mr Thrush was old, and had known Aunt Thirza for years. He liked Katrina, but frowned at the sudden appearance of her family. He had known all about their rejection of Katrina, and could see no reason for their presence now. Nor could Katrina, but she handed round tea and cucumber sandwiches and hoped that there would be enough.

The Peterses and the vicar and his wife had come back to the house too, but they had been invited... They went after half an hour, since it was apparent that the aunts and uncles intended to stay until the will had been read. On the way to the door Mrs Peters contrived to whisper that they would be back that evening, and Katrina nodded and smiled and wished with all her heart that her tiresome relations would leave.

The will was simple. Everything had been left to

Katrina—the house, and any money in Aunt Thirza's bank account. The aunts were annoyed.

'One would have thought that Thirza could have left something to her other nephews and nieces.' They pinned Mr Thrush in his chair with icy stares. 'How much did our sister leave?'

'I am not able to tell you at the moment,' he answered testily. 'And in any case, since you are not the beneficiaries, I do not see that it can be of interest to you.'

When he had gone away in his elderly motorcar they turned on Katrina. 'Lucky girl. I suppose you are going to enjoy life now, with only yourself to please. I dare say Thirza had quite a nice little sum tucked away. She always was mean…'

Katrina's flimsy hold on her good manners flew through the window. 'Don't dare to say a word about Aunt Thirza. She was as dear to me as a mother, and I loved her. She never did a mean thing or said a mean thing in her life. And what have you ever done to help her? Oh, go home, all of you! And I hope I never have to set eyes on any of you again.'

Katrina was a lovely girl; when she was in a rage she was beautiful. Now she confronted her unwanted guests, a splendid Amazon.

There was silence for a moment, and then the elder aunt said, 'Well, I'm sure we know when we are not welcome, Katrina.' She got to her feet and, followed by the rest of them, left the cottage.

Katrina shut the door on them and burst into tears. She had managed so far to keep them at bay, but now she longed for Aunt Thirza, telling her in her brisk voice to stop being such a silly girl.

She cried for a long time, until there were no tears

left, then she collected up cups, saucers and plates, washed them and tidied them away, fed Betsy, washed her own face and tidied her hair and went and sat by the moss rose. And that was where Dr Peters found her presently.

'You're coming back to us for supper,' he told her. 'Yes, yes, I know you won't stay the night, and I'll bring you back when you want, but it would be nice to talk about the funeral. Such a splendid turn-out from the village; your aunt would have appreciated that.'

So she ate her supper in the kindly company of the doctor and his wife, and afterwards the vicar and his wife came to join them and sat talking. And Katrina found to her surprise that it was quite easy to talk about the service, and the mountains of flowers and all Aunt Thirza's friends and acquaintances.

Presently the doctor drove Katrina back and saw her into the cottage. Betsy was waiting for her, and the little place was welcoming, just as though her aunt was still there. Katrina, worn out with sorrow and loneliness, went to bed and Betsy, an understanding cat, went with her.

Over the next few days the sharp end of grief was blunted by the need to get her life into some kind of order. The cottage was hers; she had a roof over her head, a roof she loved, and there would be no need for her to leave the village she loved too. She read the letter Mr Thrush sent, telling her to call at her aunt's bank and assuring her of his willingness to be of service if she needed him.

She cycled into Warminster and saw the manager, and came home again rather soberly. Aunt Thirza had a few hundred pounds in her account—enough,

as the manager had pointed out, to keep her going
for a couple of months. 'Although I dare say you
intend to find a job. You could, of course, sell the
cottage...'

'Never.' She had sounded quite fierce. 'I'll think
of something...'

She told no one about it, and to Mrs Peters' tentative question as to whether she was financially secure she said brightly that, yes, everything was fine.
When the same question was put, not out of curiosity
but out of kindness by the various friends and acquaintances living in the village, she gave the same
cheerful reassurance.

They were all so kind, asking her to lunch, to tea,
and offering lifts in their cars, calling to see her on
some pretext or other. She was grateful to them, but
it was in the evenings, when she had had her supper
and sat down with pen and paper doing sums, making plans, that her brave heart faltered. And it was
then that she wondered for the hundredth time why
the professor hadn't sent a card.

She had even dared to hope at first that he would
come and see her, but there had been no word from
him, no sign. Aunt Thirza had been one of his patients and she had died, something which he must
have experienced many times in his profession. Only
she had thought that he had liked the old lady, and
had even begun to like herself a little.

'I'm a fool, of course,' she told Betsy, and picked
up her pen once more and had another go at cutting
down expenses.

Professor Glenville, driving himself home after a
two-week tour lecturing on the continent, decided to

call in at St Aldrick's before he went home. He had come back on an early-morning hovercraft, and although he had no need to take up his duties until the following day he thought he might as well see what was lined up for him. He went to Theatre first, and had a talk with his registrar, then went to the out-patients department to let Sister know that he would be taking his clinic on the following afternoon. And, since she wasn't busy for the moment, he stopped for a cup of coffee with her.

Everything was much as usual, she told him, and then added, 'A pity about that nice old lady—Miss Gibbs—you remember her, sir? Died suddenly a week ago. Dr Peters phoned, but of course you weren't here. He asked me to let you know when you got back.'

The professor said slowly; 'I'm sorry to hear that. It was bound to happen, of course, but I had hoped that we had managed to slow her downward progress.'

He left shortly afterwards and drove to his consulting rooms, and his secretary, reed-thin, bespectacled and his devoted slave, beamed a welcome.

'There, I was only saying to Geoff'—Geoff was her husband—'that you would be back some time today. I do hope you had a successful tour, Professor.'

'Yes, thank you, Mrs Best.' He smiled down at her middle-aged face. 'Tell me, am I going to be busy next week?'

'You're booked solid, but I've kept Saturday and Sunday free.'

'Good. How am I placed for tomorrow? I'm not

due at St Aldrick's until the afternoon clinic, but have I any patients here in the morning?'

'Yes, starting at half past nine until noon. Then in the evening there are two new patients. Six-thirty and half past seven.'

Mrs Best took a look in the appointments book. 'If you wish, you could see two patients late this afternoon…'

'No, no. I'll be in tomorrow morning.' He smiled. 'I see you've been holding the fort with your usual skill.' He opened his bag and handed her a flat box. 'With my thanks!'

He was gone before she had time to give more than a hasty thanks.

It was barely eleven o'clock, and the roads were fairly quiet. He drove himself down to Wherwell, to be greeted by Peach and Mrs Peach.

'You'll be wanting a good lunch, sir,' said Peach.

The professor was halfway up the staircase. 'Peach, I have to go and see someone urgently. Would Mrs Peach cook me a splendid dinner instead, and could she make up some kind of picnic meal for me to take with me? For two.'

Peach remained impassive. 'Of course, sir. In a hurry, are you?'

'Yes. I'm going to take a shower and change—twenty minutes? And I'll take Barker and Jones with me. They're in the garden?'

In rather less than half an hour he was downstairs again, greeting the dogs before going to the kitchen to see Mrs Peach. 'I may be bringing Miss Gibbs back with me,' he told her. 'Her aunt died suddenly and I must go and see her; she might like to dine here.'

'The poor girl. Peach took quite a fancy to her—
very pretty, he said.' She put a mug of coffee down
on the kitchen table. 'You'll drink that coffee, sir,
before you go, it'll only take you a minute, and I
doubt you had a proper breakfast.'

He drank his coffee, remembering that he hadn't
actually had any breakfast, and, just as though he had
said so, Mrs Peach went on, 'There's soup, and a
cooked chicken and salad, some rolls and butter, and
Peach fetched up a bottle of that white wine you
always fancy.'

He bent and kissed her plump cheek. 'Thank you,
Mrs Peach.' When Peach saw him to the door he
said, 'I'm not sure when I shall be back. I'll phone
you if there is a change in my plans.'

He drove away, with Jones sitting beside him and
Barker on the back seat, and Peach went back to the
kitchen.

Katrina had got up early, for she had found that if
she went to bed quite late, then got up with the sun
and filled her days with gardening and cleaning the
cottage, turning out the cupboards and polishing the
brass and silver, even though it didn't need it, she
got through her days well enough for she was too
tired to think about anything much. She knew that in
time she would feel herself again, but just for a while
she needed to blot out the last two weeks.

Friends still called, of course, and when she was
invited out to a meal with them she went willingly
enough, apparently her normal rather quiet self and
quite cheerful too. They told each other that she was
a sensible girl and was getting over her aunt's death
very well. 'Seems quite content to be there on her

own,' they told each other. 'I dare say Thirza left a tidy bit in the bank, though I don't suppose Katrina will want to stay there for the rest of her life. Still, a month or two won't do her any harm. Dare say she'll find a job...'

She was in the kitchen now, sitting at the table, doing more sums. She had cycled into Warminster yesterday, intent on finding a job. She hadn't much idea how to set about it, but she had found an agency and put her name on their books, although the severe woman behind the desk had told her cuttingly that since she had no qualifications and no skills it wasn't very likely that she would find anything.

'Home help?' she had said. 'But of course you want to live out. The supermarket is wanting shelf-fillers; you could go along and ask there...'

Katrina had gone, and the manager had said flatly that she would have to work from seven in the morning until ten o'clock, and again at nine o'clock in the evening until half past ten. 'And if you don't live here in the town we wouldn't want to take you on.'

'I don't mind the hours,' Katrina had said.

He'd given her a stony look. 'Bad weather, punctured bike, overslept—too risky.' He'd turned away. 'Sorry.'

So now she was doing her sums again: such a discouraging exercise that she put her head down on her arms and cried. It didn't matter, there was no one to see, only Betsy.

The professor walked up the garden path and, since the door was open, walked in. After a moment he crossed the living room and went into the kitchen, standing in the doorway looking at Katrina's down-bent head.

He said quietly, 'Katrina?' and she looked up and then sat up quickly.

Her face was blotched with crying, but she blew her nose defiantly, wiped her eyes and wished him a polite good morning in a voice which didn't sound like hers at all.

'A cup of tea?' He appeared not to have noticed her tears and went to put the kettle on, turning his back so that she had time to scrub at her face before he came and sat down opposite her.

'I was told at the hospital this morning. I'm very sorry.'

'You've been away? You didn't know? You got back this morning?'

'Yes.'

'It must have been very early.' Katrina smiled then, and he saw that despite her sadness her spirits hadn't been broken. She said then, 'You came.' She sat up very straight. 'Aunt Thirza would have thanked you for that; I thank you too. You must be tired…and hungry.'

He got up and made the tea and put it, with mugs, milk and sugar, on the table. He said casually, 'I called in at home on my way. Mrs Peach has packed up a meal for us. While we have it you shall tell me what happened.'

He studied her face. 'Talking about it will go a long way towards making you feel better.'

She poured their tea and nodded. 'Yes, I'm sure you are right. Where have you been?'

He told her: a gentle flow of pleasant talk, making everything seem normal again, so that for the time being she forgot all about her uncertain future.

He fetched the food presently, and released the

patient dogs, having first prudently set Betsy on top of the kitchen cupboard. Katrina set the table and unpacked the food while the professor saw to the wine, before taking a bowl of water into the garden for the two dogs, and then carved the chicken.

It was all so ordinary, such an everyday way of living, thought Katrina, arranging salad, and the professor, watching her, read her thoughts. But he was careful not to be too friendly; she was unhappy and lonely now, but in a little while, when she had got over her grief, she would remember that she didn't like him overmuch. He was surprised to discover that he, on the other hand, liked her a good deal more than when they had first met.

They were both hungry, and the food was delicious, and Katrina, tossing off a second glass of wine, said happily, 'I feel quite different. I've been silly feeling sorry for myself. Aunt Thirza would have been ashamed of me.'

The professor buttered the last roll. 'You intend to live here?' he asked gently. 'I don't wish to pry, but you are in comfortable circumstances?'

Katrina answered promptly—too promptly. 'Yes, of course. Perhaps later on I shall look for something to do, but not until the summer is over.'

'Your family?'

She told him then about the aunts and uncles and cousins, taking care to make it all sound rather amusing. 'And I have such a nice solicitor to take care of everything for me.'

She hoped that sounded convincing. It had been kind of him to come and see her, especially as they hadn't been particularly friendly, but she had no wish to be beholden to him or to ask for his sympathy.

And yet she remembered that she had wanted him to come when Aunt Thirza had died. Well, she was her old self again; she would manage without anyone's help or pity.

Her thoughts made her stiffen up, and the professor noticed that. He thought that her reply to his question had been glib, but he had no reason to doubt it. It seemed a little strange that she should be so vague as to her future, but of course there was time enough for her to alter her plans. Perhaps to live here in this little cottage among her friends and where she was well-known *was* the best thing for the moment. Anyway, it really was no business of his.

He sensed that she wanted him to go. Without seeming to make haste, he helped her put the remains of their meal back in the box, whistled to the dogs and went out to the car. Katrina went with him, and when he had stowed the box and the dogs she offered a hand.

'Thank you for coming,' she said in an over-bright voice. 'I'm sorry I was so silly—there's been a lot to do, and I dare say I'm a bit tired. I'm really looking forward to the rest of the summer. I hope...' What did she hope? She had no idea. 'You'll be glad to get home. Thank you for helping Aunt Thirza. I'll always be grateful. Goodbye, Professor...'

He took her hand. 'You are most fortunate to have people you know living near you, and so many friends. Enjoy your summer. I'm sure you will find something you want to do later on—or you might marry.'

She said bleakly, 'I don't know anyone—any men, that is. Only married ones or elderly gentlemen.' And then at his intent look she added brightly, 'There's always Mr Right waiting round the corner, isn't there?'

She laughed, to let him see how cheerfully she viewed the future.

'Indeed—especially if he is looking for a pretty girl with her own home and the means to live in it in comfort.' He smiled then. 'Take care, Katrina, not to marry a fortune-hunter.'

She watched him drive away. She wouldn't see him again, of course. She would never know if he married, if he was happy. Perhaps Dr Peters would hear of him from time to time; she could always ask him. But there would be no point in doing that. He had come into her life on a mere whim of Fate, and gone again just when she had realised that she liked him after all.

She went back indoors, fed Betsy and, since it was far too early to have supper, made a pot of tea and sat down again with pen and paper. She would make a list of the things she could do, and take care to study the local paper each week and see what kinds of job were advertised. She was a bit limited; it would have to be near enough for her to bike to work and it would have to be something within her scope.

Children? she wondered. Looking after someone elderly? Helping on a farm? The last possibility pleased her. There were farms all round the village; there must be potatoes to dig, sprouts to pick, soft fruit...

Immensely cheered, she went to bed early. She could afford to spend another month or six weeks being idle, seeing her friends, helping with the bazaar and fête, allaying the doubts of some of the older friends of her aunt, who suspected that there was very little money, and then finding work with the casual labourers.

That would do for a start, she told herself sleepily. If she could make enough money to keep her going through the winter she could study at home and go to evening classes in Warminster, and then, armed with a diploma or two, get a secure job—typing, or being a receptionist, or a dental nurse. Her head full of ideas, she slept.

She woke early, and her first unbidden thought was of the professor, driving himself up to St Aldrick's. She told herself that there was no point in thinking about him. He was someone from the past; it was the future which mattered now.

# CHAPTER FOUR

DRIVING home, Professor Glenville had thought about Katrina. He had had every intention of taking her back to his home for supper but she had made it very obvious that she would have refused to come. For a little while she had seemed happier, and then, when he had mentioned her plans for the future, she had answered him in a voice which had dared him to ask any more questions. Indeed, she had seemed glad to see him go.

Peach, coming into the hall as he'd gone in, had wished him good evening.

'The young lady isn't with you, sir?'

'No, Peach. Will you convey her thanks to Mrs Peach? The lunch was delicious.' He'd paused at his study door. 'I'll take the dogs for a run...'

'You'd like tea first, sir?' Peach had asked.

'When I get back, Peach. Half an hour?'

He'd whistled to the dogs and gone down the garden and into the fields beyond. Perhaps he should have ignored Katrina's sudden coolness and stayed longer; good manners would have forced her to offer him tea, and perhaps he could have coaxed whatever was worrying her into the open. She had been distinctly cagey. On the other hand she might have felt his visit to be an intrusion.

He'd been wryly amused that he should feel concern for her, for she'd shown little inclination to be more than polite. Only when he had found her in tears he had had a strong wish to comfort her and had had a glimpse of an unhappy girl. Probably she wished that the brief moment when they had been close had never occurred.

He'd gone back to the house presently, to eat his tea and then to immerse himself in work, Katrina forgotten.

He went to work in his consulting rooms in the morning, and then on to the hospital to take his clinic. His registrar was waiting for him—a rather silent man, younger than the professor. They had worked together for some years and were good friends.

'It's a large clinic, I'm afraid,' he told him. 'We've been saving them up until you got back! Young Taylor's settled in nicely. You asked for a fourth member of the team. She joined us last week. A girl, Maureen Soames. Quite good and very keen.'

They went together to Outpatients and found Sister waiting for them. Taylor was there too, a bright young doctor, keen to specialise, and beside him the new member of the team. She was a small dark girl, with short curly hair and large dark eyes in an attractive face. She was slim, and her smile was charming as she shook hands.

The professor thought that she didn't look old enough to be qualified, let alone specialise; she should be doing what other girls did—shopping, dancing, playing tennis with a string of young men. She looked fragile, the kind of girl who needed a man to look after her. He smiled at her kindly and hoped that she would be happy with his team before going to his consulting room with Sister.

The clinic lasted longer than usual, and he was on

the point of leaving when Maureen came to the door. 'I wondered if you could spare a moment, sir? This Mrs Wiseman—I know she's an old patient, and holding her own nicely, but I'm not sure that I understand why you ordered that particular treatment…'

The professor put down his bag. 'You have her notes? Then let us sit down for a few minutes and I will explain.'

It didn't take long. Presently they walked through the hospital together and parted at the entrance, and the professor, watching her walk away, reflected that Maureen Soames was a charming girl as well as a clever one. Which was exactly what she had intended him to think.

After the professor's visit Katrina, feeling lonely, spent her time in the garden. There was plenty to do there. The ground he had dug was already planted with sprouts and cabbages, carrots and turnips. At least she would always have vegetables. She worked every day until she was tired, and then went indoors and made tea. She sat thinking about the professor, wishing that she could see him again, but of course that wouldn't happen. He had come to see her out of kindness, and because he had liked Aunt Thirza. Probably he felt relief at the idea of a duty fulfilled.

Still, tomorrow was another day, she told herself. She had promised to help get the stalls ready for the bazaar, to be held in the middle of next week. But it was of the professor she was thinking when at last she fell asleep.

For as long as Katrina could remember Aunt Thirza had presided over the ladies who, each year, organised the church bazaar, and now, although she had nothing to do with the committee, it was taken for granted that *she* would take over the more mundane tasks. So her next few days were fully occupied collecting the hats, dresses and unwanted handbags from the better-off inhabitants, pricing them and arranging them just so under the eagle eyes of the matrons in charge of the bazaar. There were also books to collect, bric-a-brac to wash and polish, bottles to collect for the bottle stall; for the moment she put aside her worries and plans.

The day of the bazaar brought warm sunshine, and Katrina, in one of her pretty but no longer fashionable frocks, was at the Manor House early, helping to arrange the stalls on the lawn, fetching and carrying, making herself useful. Lady Truscott, who owned the manor, was to open the bazaar at eleven o'clock, and Katrina and Mrs Peters were rearranging a last-minute display of hats.

'So kind,' said Mary Peters, 'allowing us to use her lawn each year. A pity she has no family. Though there's a niece, I believe. A clever girl, I'm told, on the staff at St Aldrick's.'

She laid down the last of the hats. 'Here comes Lady Truscott. Oh, that's her niece with her. Pretty, isn't she?'

Katrina agreed. Any girl would look pretty in that silk suit, but she had to admit that the girl was rather more than pretty—elegant, self-assured, probably with a string of young men. Katrina wondered what it would be like to have a string of young men...

Lady Truscott and her niece began a tour of the stalls, buying egg cosies, crocheted mats and woolly toys. They were hardly expected to buy anything from the second-hand stall, but they paused for a few words.

'You don't know my niece?' asked Lady Truscott. 'Maureen Soames—the clever girl is a doctor, you know, specialising in haematology—Professor Glenville's team. He thinks highly of her.' Lady Truscott looked smug. 'By all accounts they are great friends…'

Maureen assumed a look of modest protest but she smiled, a small secret smile which annoyed Katrina. The girl was putting on an act… Katrina didn't like her, and she hoped that all this talk of being great friends with the professor was nonsense.

She said now, 'You must be very clever. Have you a day off or are you on holiday?'

Maureen gave her a limpid look. 'Oh, only a day. The professor works us hard.' She gave a tinkling laugh. 'But we contrive to enjoy ourselves too! I must go back shortly; we're going out this evening.'

'Burning the candle at both ends?' asked Katrina lightly. 'I suppose I can't interest you in a hat?'

The look that Maureen gave her was a clear indication that they weren't to be friends.

When they had gone Mrs Peters said comfortably, 'Now, isn't that nice? I liked the professor, didn't you? How delightful if he were to fall in love with Maureen. Such a pretty girl, and they do say that big men always fall for dainty little creatures like Maureen.'

That was the kind of remark which made Katrina feel outsize, and clumsy to boot.

The day over, the stalls packed up, the money counted, she went back home, refusing Mrs Peters' invitation to supper, saying that she had a lot to do that evening. Betsy met her, anxious for her supper, and presently Katrina boiled an egg, made toast and a pot of tea and sat down at the table to eat it. It had been a busy day, and very successful, only not very happy.

Meeting Maureen had brought the memory of the professor back with a vengeance, just when she was beginning to forget him. But it seemed that he wasn't to be consigned to the past; she might not see him again, but from time to time she would be given tit-bits of news about him, since Mrs Peters and Lady Truscott were friendly enough to exchange gossip.

'Serve him right if he marries her,' said Katrina unfairly, and not meaning a word of it. Maureen might be pretty and beautifully dressed, but under that charming exterior there lurked a young woman bent on getting her own way. 'She's out to catch the professor,' said Katrina, so loudly that Betsy woke up and looked at her. 'Sorry, Betsy, I didn't mean to disturb you. But he'll never be happy with her.'

Which, when she thought about it, was a silly thing to say; she hardly knew him, and she had no idea of his private life, his likes and dislikes. Very likely he admired small, dainty women, especially when they were clever doctors. 'Oh well,' said Katrina vaguely, and put herself to bed.

She got up early, determined to finish planting up the garden and then cycle over to Mr Thorn's farm and see if he needed casual labour. He was far enough from the village to preclude the chance of anyone there finding out that she had a job at the farm. She didn't mind them knowing, but she shrank from their pity and concern and offers of help...

But help was something she was going to need;

there was a letter on the doormat when she went downstairs, and it was an outstanding bill which had been overlooked. It was overdue, and obviously Aunt Thirza had forgotten to pay it. This, she read, was a final demand, and would Miss Gibbs be good enough to forward the amount owing immediately?

It wasn't a great deal of money, but it would make a sizeable hole in her bank account. She wrote a cheque and a letter of explanation and went down to the village to post it. There were more customers than usual in Mrs Dyer's shop, and Katrina had to wait for a while until Mrs Dyer could cast off her mantle of shopkeeper and assume the mental cloak of the post office.

'Did well with the bazaar this year, I hear,' she observed, handing over stamps. 'The weather was a treat too. My Amy bought one of those hats—the pink straw. She's going to a friend's wedding next week, and no one there will know where she got it.'

'The pink straw? That was one of Lady Truscott's—very expensive—Amy's got a bargain!'

'There now. There's talk about her niece. Amy said she is as pretty as a picture and a doctor and all...works at St Aldrick's. I dare say you didn't meet her when you went there with Miss Gibbs? She's with some well-known professor. He's sweet on her, so they say.'

'They?' asked Katrina, in what she hoped was a casual manner.

'Well, you know how it is, Miss Katrina. A word here and a word there.' Mrs Dyer laughed cosily. 'Never smoke without fire.' She handed over the change. 'You met that professor, didn't you? Handsome man, so I'm told.'

'Yes, yes, he is. He was very kind to my aunt. I believe he's very clever.'

Mrs Dyer, with no other customer there, was disposed to chat. 'Settled down nicely, have you, love? I dare say you'll be off to see a bit of the world once things have settled down.'

'Well, perhaps, but I plan to stay at Rose Cottage for the rest of the summer. I couldn't possibly leave the garden.'

'Not lonely there, are you?' Mrs Dyer beamed at her. 'Let's hope some nice young man will come along and marry you.'

Katrina laughed with her, bought a tin of Betsy's favourite cat food and went back home. She had had to waste a good deal of the morning. It would be best if she did some gardening now and hung out the washing, then had an early lunch and went to Thorn's Farm afterwards.

The farm was four miles away, and when Aunt Thirza had been alive Katrina had often cycled over to fetch a chicken or a turkey. It was a prosperous place, with a vast apple orchard and several acres of soft fruit as well as surrounding fields with crops of potatoes, beans and cabbages.

Mr Thorn was in his greenhouse, inspecting the tomato plants. He was a taciturn man, and he listened to her without comment, then said, 'Can't say I blame you, young lady, for wanting to stay on at Rose Cottage. Nice little property, and Miss Thirza took good care of it. Didn't leave much, I suppose?' He didn't wait for her answer. 'It just so happens that I could do with a bit of extra help. Broad beans—must get 'em picked while the weather holds.'

He glanced at Katrina's hands—nicely shaped and well cared for. 'It's rough on your hands…'

'When can I start?' asked Katrina.

'Soon as you like. As to pay; the more you pick the more you earn. Up to you. Mostly they start at eight o'clock and work mornings, but you can work on until five or six o'clock if you've a mind. Reckon it'll be a good week's work. And if the weather holds, there'll be the peas next.'

'I'll be here at eight o'clock,' said Katrina, and cycled home, where she sat down once more to do her sums. If she worked for four days a week she could add considerably to the diminishing bank account, and, since she could pick and choose when she worked, she could still carry on with normal living on the other days: the church flowers, the occasional tennis party, helping with the summer fête… It wasn't that she was too proud to tell anyone that she was going to work at the farm, but if they suspected that she was having difficulties making ends meet they would want to help…

It worked out very well. Getting up early was no hardship; she would have breakfast, feed Betsy, make sandwiches for her lunch and get on her bike. It was hard work, she hadn't realised how hard, but at the end of the day she went back home with money in her pocket. Aching all over, she would eat supper, with Betsy for company, before soaking away the aches in a hot bath and dealing with her roughened hands to present herself, in a cotton dress, her hair neatly coiled, the hands passable, at one or other of the committee meetings which took up so much of village life. She was much in demand—to write up the minutes, arrange dates, put leaflets through letterboxes...

Her friends, mostly older ladies who had been friends of her aunt, nodded their rigidly permed heads and told each other that Katrina had settled down nicely and it was to be hoped that she would meet a nice man and marry. Indeed, several of them with likely nephews engineered meetings in the hope that Katrina would fall in love with one of them, but although she was friendly, played tennis with them, and cheerfully accompanied them on walks or visits to Warminster, she remained heart-whole.

They made a nice change from the farm, and she was grateful for youthful company, but that was all. She had no intention of marrying, she told herself. First she must get her life organised; the nest egg was growing nicely, and by the end of the summer she would be able to go to evening classes at Warminster and train—shorthand, typing and computers, and once she had mastered these, the world—or at least the country towns within bus or bike distance—would be her oyster. And always at the back of her mind was the professor who, despite her best efforts, refused to be consigned to the past.

There hadn't been much rain, so the pea crop didn't last long, but by then the potatoes were ready. It was a back-breaking job, and ruinous for the hands even though she wore gloves, and then on the days when the strawberry crop was ready they had to be picked at once, which was also a back-breaking job in the hot summer days. But Katrina had got into her stride now. She worked all the hours she was allowed, and became tanned by the sun, but she was getting thin, and very tired at the end of the day. But the nest egg grew!

One or two of her friends in the village had remarked about her new slimness, and wondered out loud why her hands were no longer well kept.

'It's the garden,' she explained airily. 'There's such a lot to do, and I do enjoy it. I spend hours out of doors, grubbing around. I must go to Warminster and treat myself to a manicure.'

It was the day before the fête, and she intended to work an extra hour or so at the farm so that she could be free on the following day. Aunt Thirza had always been a leading light at the fête, and Katrina had always helped her and spent the following day helping with the clearing up. She must do the same this year too. It was a splendid morning, and once at the farm she worked with a will in the strawberry field, on her hands and knees amongst the luscious fruit. She was sitting under a hedge eating her sandwiches with several other workers when Mr Thorn came across to them.

'Katrina? You're planning to work until five o'clock?' When she nodded he said, 'Lady Truscott wants six pounds of strawberries for this evening. Can you take them down on your bike? Go a bit earlier—I'll pay you up to five o'clock.'

He didn't wait for her reply but walked away. Although he was fair in his dealings with his workers she knew he would chalk up a bad mark against her if she refused. She would go along the back drive to the Manor House and hand the strawberries in at the kitchen door. She had no wish to meet Lady Truscott.

She had to go about a mile out of her way, and it was a warm afternoon. The back drive was long and, since it was seldom used, full of ruts and pot holes. She wobbled along on her bike, the strawberries in their box tied on her carrier. She was thinking about the fête on the morrow. She would wear her prettiest dress, a cream and amber crêpe with elbow-length sleeves and a prim collar. Aunt Thirza had given it to her several years ago and it was only worn on special occasions. It was quite out of date of course, but it was elegant, and so seldom on view that she hoped people would think it was new.

She was to be in charge of the bottle stall, which meant being there early in the morning since the fête opened at eleven o'clock. People came from surrounding villages, trooping up and down the narrow main street where the stalls were erected, buying balloons for the children, choosing second-hand books and looking at the splendid collection of bric-a-brac. And besides these delights there was a roundabout for the children, lotteries and, of course, the bottle stall.

The back drive wound round the Manor's small park to join the main drive at the front of the house, which meant that Katrina would have to pedal across the front sweep and down the other side to the kitchen entrance. She reached the fork and looked each way. There was no one in sight. Lady Truscott would be having tea, either in the drawing room which overlooked the ornamental garden at the back or in the garden itself.

She shot across the front of the house, and almost at its far corner the Bentley swept past her, with the professor at the wheel and a very pretty dark girl sitting beside him. She swerved round the side of the house and stopped at the kitchen entrance, furious

with herself because she was shaking. He might not
have seen her, and even if he had she looked quite
unlike her usual self.

She handed over the strawberries and went cautiously back to the corner of the house. The Bentley
was parked in front of the door but there was no sign
of anyone. She got on her bike, thinking if she went
fast she could be round the first bend of the main
drive before anyone who happened to be looking out
of any of the windows saw her. And that was unlikely for they would be having tea...

The professor, standing with Maureen in the hall
by the open door, saw her. And so did Maureen.

'Who is that?' she asked, and looked round for
someone to tell her since the professor wasn't likely
to know. 'What a scarecrow—from one of the farms,
I suppose.' She smiled up at him. 'Are you sure you
can't stay—just half an hour or so?'

He had nice manners. His refusal was polite but
firm and he got into his car and drove away. He
overtook Katrina as she turned out of the park into
the lane. Rose Cottage was the best part of a mile
ahead of her and when she reached it the Bentley
was parked in front of the gate and he was leaning
over it.

As she got off her bike he said cheerfully, 'Hello,
am I in time for tea?'

He opened the gate and she went past him. She
said, in a polite voice which hid a mixture of pleasure
at seeing him again and annoyance that they had met
when she was looking at her worst, 'Do come in. I'll
put the kettle on.'

She unlocked the door and led the way into the

kitchen. 'I dare say you're anxious to get back to town.'

'Now why should you say that? I have the whole evening before me.'

'Oh, you're going back to the Manor?'

'No. Why have you got thinner, Katrina? And why do you look tired and work-weary? And your hands...'

She said flatly, 'I haven't had time to wash and change.' She thumped the sugar bowl down upon the table and bent to offer Betsy a saucer of milk. 'If I had known that you intended to visit me I would have been prepared!'

He poured the tea and sat down when she did. 'You had better tell me, Katrina.'

'Tell you what? And I don't intend to anyway; it's none of your business.'

'Just so. We will start again. What were you doing at the Manor, looking like a scarecrow? I seem to remember that your aunt was friendly with Lady Truscott. So why were you skulking round the kitchen quarters pretending that you weren't there?'

'I was not skulking; I was delivering some fruit. Of course I know Lady Truscott; I just didn't want to meet her then.'

He picked up the hand by her mug. 'And your hands—working on a farm, Katrina?'

'And why shouldn't I, if I want to? It's—it's delightful out of doors...'

'Grubbing up potatoes, picking peas and strawberries?'

It was annoying, the way he was hitting the nail on the head. She decided not to answer.

The professor said slowly, 'You won't tell me, so

I will tell you. You're on your beam ends, aren't you? Rose Cottage is yours, but you have no money, although everyone thinks that your aunt left you well provided for. You don't want them to know that, do you? You loved her, didn't you? And she would have been upset to have left you penniless. So you lead two lives. The village think of you as Miss Katrina Gibbs, left in comfortable circumstances by one of the most respected people living here, while you grub a living at some farm sufficiently far away for no one to know anything about it.'

She sat silent, because she could think of nothing to say and there was no point in denying it.

He sat back watching her, and presently she said in a polite voice, 'It's the summer fête tomorrow; I'm in charge of the bottle stall.' And then, 'I didn't know that you were acquainted with Lady Truscott.'

'I'm not. Maureen Soames, who is on my team, begged a lift. Her car broke down and she had promised to be here for this fête. She is Lady Truscott's niece.'

'She's a doctor, isn't she? You're staying at the Manor?'

He hid a smile. 'No.' He ate the last biscuit in the tin. 'I must go—I need to be home this evening.' He got to his feet and she stood up.

'Yes, of course. Thank you for calling in.' She offered a hand and he felt how very rough it was in his.

They walked to the gate together; it was still warm, a lovely evening, with a blue sky turning rose and golden at its edges. It was very quiet, and there was a honeysuckle rambling along the hedge, smelling sweetly.

The professor's handsome nose twitched. 'I can smell verbena...'

'Yes, Aunt Thirza loved it. I can remember it being here when I came here to live.'

He nodded. 'It should be a splendid day for your fête.'

He got into the car, lifted a hand and drove away. She stood at the gate for quite a while, and then went indoors and began on the task of restoring her hands to some kind of smoothness. The little house seemed very empty without him.

The village was a hive of activity when Katrina reached the main street. Stalls were being erected, crates of lemonade, boxes of food, books and china were being unpacked and arranged. It was already eight o'clock and there was a lot to do...

The ladies of the village greeted her warmly.

'Pretty as a picture,' said Mrs Dyer to the butcher's wife, 'and ever so smart in that dress. Keeps herself to herself, mind, but then so did Miss Gibbs. Pity there's no young man, but it's early days and she can pick and choose. Rose Cottage is a snug little place, and I dare say Miss Gibbs left her comfortable.'

They both turned to look at Katrina across the street, arranging bottles on her stall. 'She's got a bit thin, but there, she's had a sad time of it.'

Katrina labelled bottles, arranged them in tidy rows and exchanged gossip with everyone there. It was Mrs Tripp, taking a few hours off from her nursing duties, who called across to her.

'I'll have to go before lunch; Dr Peters wants me to run out to the Stokeses—Mrs Stokes is a bit poorly. Hope I get a chance to see that niece of Lady Truscott. I hear she's quite something, pretty and ever so smart. Come down specially to be at the fête with her aunt. Came by car—a Bentley, too. The man with her was a bit of a sensation, so Cook from the manor told me. Giant of a fellow, very good-looking. Made a splendid pair, she said.'

Katrina bent over her bottles. 'Let's hope you'll get a chance to see her before you have to go.'

She was glad that she had something to do; the bottles needed to be cunningly placed: the bottle of whisky and the three bottles of wine well to the fore, flanked by the brown sauce and the tomato ketchup. Someone had donated a great many bottles of cola, which made a good show, but there were also bottles of vinegar, mouthwash and half a dozen bottles of shower gel—obviously unwanted presents left over from Christmas, which needed to be tucked away behind the more exciting prizes.

People were beginning to trickle down the street. They were unable to buy anything until the fête was opened, but they went from stall to stall, earmarking what they hoped to buy once the speeches had been made.

This year a TV personality was to start the proceedings. Katrina, who almost never went to the cinema and no longer had the TV her aunt had rented, was a bit vague as to who he was, but as the party from the Manor arrived, and he with them, she craned her neck to look like everyone else.

He looked like anyone else, she thought disappointedly, and his speech was much too long and flowery, but it gave her the chance to take a good look at the niece. She was, indeed, pretty as a picture.

Her cream silk shift was so short that there didn't seem much point in wearing it, as Mrs Tripp whispered to Katrina, but her hat was a breathtaking affair: a dipping brim of straw with a wealth of roses around its crown. Katrina, edging a little nearer, saw that she was beautifully made up and that the dark hair under the hat was short and curling. She stood, looking round her, smiling a little—as if, thought Katrina, she was secretly amused at this rural ritual.

I don't like her, reflected Katrina, ignoring several more reasons why she didn't.

The speeches over at last, the business of the day began. Everyone was out to enjoy themselves. The children were all there, and the outlying farmers' wives, who only went to the village or the nearest town on market days, were there. And so were the elderly retired folk who lived in the larger houses on the fringe of the village.

Katrina, replenishing her stock from her prudent cache behind the stall, was doing a roaring trade. It was when the small crowd around the stall parted that she came face to face with Lady Truscott and her niece.

Lady Truscott had a rather loud voice. She said, with the tactlessness for which she was renowned, 'My dear Katrina, I see you're carrying on your aunt's good work. Such a pity that she should die— and so unexpectedly.'

She became aware of the sudden silence around her and hurried on, 'May I have some tickets, if you can spare them?'

She turned to Maureen. 'You remember Katrina Gibbs, dear—you met at the bazaar.

'Maureen was given a lift here by Professor

Glenville, Katrina. Of course you met him when he attended your dear aunt.'

Katrina flashed a smile at Maureen. 'Hello again. You must have an interesting job. Are you staying here long?'

Maureen didn't bother to smile. She said sharply, 'I have to be on duty tomorrow morning—the professor's clinic. I'm kept very busy.'

Katrina handed over the tickets, and while Lady Truscott unfolded them observed casually, 'Well, London isn't far off, is it? Did you come by train or drive down?'

'Oh, Simon—Professor Glenville—brought me.' She gave Katrina a puzzled look. 'My aunt said so just now. It's no distance in his car.'

Maureen thought it a good thing that this aunt had died; Katrina was lovely, if in a large way. The professor might have found her attractive. Luckily there was no need for him to see her again.

'I suppose I'd better have a couple of tickets,' she said ungraciously.

Katrina sold her two, and hoped that she wouldn't get anything at all or, even better, something dull, like a bottle of vinegar. Her hope was justified; Maureen won a garish bottle of shower gel of an unknown make and handed it back with a sneering little laugh. 'Not quite my style.'

'But you did win,' Katrina pointed out sweetly.

Maureen stared at her. 'I always win,' she said.

Katrina was pleasantly tired when she got back to Rose Cottage that evening.

The clearing up in the village street had been a mammoth task, but a cheerful one. Everyone was pleased; almost everything had been sold, eaten or drunk, and the profits would be good. The church tower fund would benefit, as it always did, and the few shops had done a roaring trade. She had gone back with Mrs Peters and had supper with her and the doctor, and Mrs Peters had had a great deal to say about the fête.

The doctor had listened idly. 'The Manor House party was there, I suppose? What was the TV chap like?'

'He looked like everyone else,' said Katrina. 'A bit disappointing.'

'And was Lady Truscott's niece there? She's a very attractive girl.' He glanced at Katrina. 'Did you know that Professor Glenville drove her down?'

Katrina speared a bit of sausage. 'Yes, he called to see me on his way back. He didn't stay…' She popped the sausage in her mouth.

'He came to see me too,' the doctor said. 'Says you're too thin.'

Katrina went pink. 'Did he indeed? I never felt better, and I was getting fat…'

'Just right,' said Mrs Peters comfortably. 'It isn't my business, my dear, but why don't you have a nice holiday? A cruise, or stay at a good hotel by the sea, and when you come back join a few things—Warminster has a very good amateur dramatic society, or you could join a swimming club, and I believe Miss Grimm is going to start pottery classes in the autumn.'

Katrina said brightly, 'I must certainly think about that, but it's so pleasant at the cottage in the summer, and I've got my hands full in the garden.'

She thanked them for her supper and the doctor took her home.

'Well, you can have a nice quiet day tomorrow,' he observed.

She remembered that she had said that she would be at the farm by seven o'clock in the morning. 'Oh, yes, I shall,' she assured him, and kissed his elderly cheek.

'There's something not quite right,' said the doctor when he got back home. 'I don't know what it is.' He yawned, for he had had a long day. 'We will have to wait and see.'

Professor Glenville, eating his solitary dinner, decided that he wasn't going to wait and see. He told himself that he had no personal interest in Katrina, but felt it his duty to help her if he could. But how?

He was interrupted in his thoughts by Peach, coming to tell him that Miss Soames was on the phone. His 'Glenville' was abrupt enough to make her pause, but only for a moment.

'I've missed my train, and my aunt has gone out to dinner and taken the car. I hate to ask you, but please could you come and fetch me, Professor?'

His reply was even more abrupt. 'Impossible. I'm going to the hospital now. Get a taxi.' And then, remembering his manners, he added, 'I'm sorry.'

# CHAPTER FIVE

THE professor, bidding his team a civil good morning before they set off on their ward round, wondered if he had been a little terse with Maureen when she had phoned him, but apparently not; she returned his greeting with a sunny smile and followed it with a sensible question about the first patient. Nor did she bother him with details as to how she'd got back home the previous evening.

Perhaps he should have driven down to fetch her, he reflected. If he hadn't been so preoccupied with Katrina he might have done so. He frowned; he mustn't allow the girl to intrude into his busy life; Katrina had been ungracious, to say the least.

Nevertheless, as the days slipped by, he found that she wasn't easy to forget.

Strolling around his lovely garden with the dogs in the evenings, he wondered about her; was she really happy at Rose Cottage with just Betsy for company? And how long was she going to keep up the pretence of being comfortably off? The long winter evenings would be lonely, and even if she found work she would go home to an empty house of an evening...

It was ten days after the fête that he went home a little earlier than usual, requested Mrs Peach to serve his dinner, and, having eaten it, whistled the dogs, ushered them into the car and drove to Rose Cottage.

He doubted that Katrina would be pleased to see

him, and he had no doubt that she would cavil at his suggestion, but he had spent time and thought on it since the solution to her problem had revealed itself. If she would agree, nothing could be more satisfactory. It had been while he was examining one of his small patients with leukaemia, a little girl of eight who had responded well to chemotherapy, that he'd known what he wanted to do. Tracey and her widowed mother lived in a high-rise block of flats near St Aldrick's; to transport them both to the country for a few months would be ideal. They could have a quiet life, good food and regular check-ups, which would give him the chance to visit Rose Cottage.

He would have to tread warily, cook up some story about the NHS paying their keep—he had taken care to discover the kind of payment that might be made—and stress the need for Tracey to be given a chance to recover completely. Katrina, under her sometimes frosty exterior, had a very soft and warm heart; he wasn't sure how he knew that but he did!

Dusk was falling when he arrived at Rose Cottage; it was still warm and the flowers in the garden smelled sweet. The door was shut and there were no lights. He walked down the garden and found Katrina on her knees planting winter spinach.

When she saw him she scrambled to her feet. 'Oh—oh, it's you,' she said. A silly thing to say, but she had been thinking about him and there he was, looking self-assured and slightly amused. 'Is there something the matter?'

'No, no. Have I startled you? Do you always associate me with disaster?'

She shook her head. 'I wasn't expecting you—anyone—to call.'

He glanced around him. 'The garden looks charming. I suppose you don't get much time during the day...'

Katrina picked up her dibber and the empty basket. She said baldly, 'I don't work for Mr Thorn any more. He's had to cut back, and the others have families.'

'That's splendid news.'

'What a horrid thing to say. I don't know why you've come, but if it's to annoy me you can go away again.'

'Tut-tut, you're being hasty, and, since I'm here, the least you can do is offer me a cup of coffee.'

'Oh, well, all right.' Then, curiosity getting the better of her peevishness, she asked, 'Are you staying at the Manor?'

'No.' He took the basket from her and put it in the shed, and when they went indoors he filled the kettle and put it on the gas with the air of a man who knew his way around the place.

Katrina got mugs and the coffee, and put a tin of biscuits on the table. They were the last she had, and she had been saving them in case someone should visit her from the village. She gave the tin a little shake, and counted them, and the professor saw that; he had also seen the neat and almost empty cupboard when he had looked for the sugar.

He asked casually, 'So, you don't work for Thorn any more?'

'Not for the last three days.' She added defiantly, 'It's nice to have the days free.' And, because she wanted to convince him of that said, 'There's always something to do in the garden, and then there's al-

ways something or other in the village, and the flowers for the church...'

He put their mugs on the table and pulled out her
chair before going to sit down opposite her.

'Don't try so hard, Katrina.' At her furious look
he added, 'And don't fly off the handle before you
have heard what I want to say to you. I need your
help...'

'Me? You want me to help you?'

'Exactly. Just forget that you don't like me, because that has nothing to do with what I'm going to
ask of you. If you will sit quietly and listen without
interrupting...'

He told her about Tracey in a calm, unhurried
manner, his voice quiet and detached. 'She deserves
a chance,' he told her. 'She's a nice child, and her
mother is a quiet woman who needs a friend. The
allowance for the two of them is adequate. Not over-
generous, but it's the going rate. I'd like them to stay
for two or three months, perhaps longer, while I try
to get them into a different flat through the Social
Services. If you dislike the idea, say so. You may
have other plans, or dislike the idea of having someone here with you, in which case I'll say no more
about it.'

'What made you think of me?' asked Katrina.

He smiled. 'Tracey was telling me how very much
she wanted a cat, but of course they are unable to
have a pet where they live. I remembered Betsy then.

'I've taken up too much of your time.' He got to
his feet, and Barker and Jones, sitting beside his
chair, rose with him.

Katrina sat where she was, looking at him. Why
did he keep harping on the fact that she disliked him?

Because she didn't—she might have done to begin
with, but not any more. He would make a marvellous
friend. If she wasn't careful she would be pouring
out her worries and woes all over his shoulders…

'I think I would like Tracey and her mother to
come here. I'm—I'm sometimes a little lonely, and
I need the money. But supposing they don't like me?'

He smiled then. 'Unlikely, but if they don't want
to stay we'll sort that problem out when it arises.
You have no objections to me telling Dr Peters? I
should like him to know about Tracey, although I
shall come down from time to time to give her a
check-up.'

Katrina got up then. 'Will you let me know when
they are coming?'

'Yes. It will be within the week. Tracey has just
had a check-up and I won't need to see her for some
time.'

A remark which left Katrina feeling disappointed,
although she told herself she had no reason to be—
the reverse, in fact, for her problems for the imme-
diate future had been solved. Beyond that didn't matter for the moment.

The professor went away shortly, careful to keep
to his pleasant, detached manner. 'You'll hear from
my secretary very shortly,' he assured her, shook
hands and took himself off.

When she could no longer see the car's tail-lights,
and everything round her was quiet again, Katrina
went back indoors and upstairs to her aunt's bedroom.

It was the largest of the two rooms, and furnished
with an old-fashioned dressing table and wardrobe,
and a rather splendid bed which had belonged to

Aunt Thirza's parents. She stood in the middle of the room, vexed that she hadn't told the professor that the cottage was really only meant for two people. Unless, of course, the child slept with her mother. But it was a pleasant place, and with a few flowers, and a book or two by the bed, and perhaps a tin of biscuits... Her own room was smaller, with a single bed, another old-fashioned wardrobe and dressing table, and the patchwork counterpane her aunt had patiently sewn over the years.

She must remember to ask about the beds, thought Katrina, going downstairs to sit at the table once more with pencil and paper, doing sums—much more optimistic now. She didn't expect to save any of the allowance she would receive, not if she were to feed her guests well, but it did mean that she wouldn't need to buy food for herself, so that her bank account need not be touched. And the allowance, the professor had mentioned casually, also covered the cost of lighting and heating, and general wear and tear.

The village would ask questions, of course but, even if curious, they were kind-hearted people, and would see nothing strange in her offering a home to a sick child and her mother. Not that Katrina would have minded if they saw fit to think otherwise.

The next day she packed the small possessions belonging to her aunt and put them in the old-fashioned chest in the tiny cubbyhole under the stairs, then cleaned out the cupboards and drawers, hung the blanket and quilt outside in the bright sunshine and polished everything so that the room no longer looked as if it belonged to Aunt Thirza. Then she wondered if she had been a fool to count her chickens before they hatched. The professor could for some reason or other change his mind.

But he hadn't. There was a letter in the morning, not from him but from his secretary, setting out on paper everything he had told her. And would she be prepared to receive her lodgers in four days' time? Her reply would be appreciated.

She sat down and wrote her answer at once, and went along to Mrs Dyer to post it. At the same time she shut herself in the village phone box and dealt with the question of the bed. The secretary sounded nice; it was something she would deal with at once, she assured Katrina, but she thought it likely that Tracey and her mother would have no objection to sharing it. 'They live in a dreadful poky place, twelve storeys up—I've been there with Professor Glenville—and they were sharing a single bed.'

Katrina thanked her. The secretary had a pretty voice; perhaps she was a pretty woman. She would, of course, see a great deal of the professor. The thought was vaguely disquieting, although she dismissed it as nonsense. And why on earth should she mind if the man had a dozen pretty secretaries?

Tracey and her mother were to arrive in time for lunch; Katrina supposed that they would travel by train and get a bus or a taxi to the village. She was up early, arranging fresh flowers, making a salad, putting coffee and lemonade ready in case they arrived earlier. She was upstairs, making a final inspection, when the professor called up the stairs, 'Anyone at home?'

When she came galloping down the stairs he said, 'We're early...'

She hadn't expected him. 'I didn't know you would be bringing Tracey...'

He smiled. 'I didn't tell you, did I? Are you pleased to see me, Katrina?'

She was delighted, but she hoped it didn't show. 'You are always welcome, Professor,' she said in a composed voice. She peered over his shoulder.

'Tracey is with you? And her mother?'

'Yes, may I fetch them? They're excited and nervous. Mrs Ward has had a hard time of it for the last year or so. I believe you to be just the person to help her regain her pleasure in life.'

He went back to the car and presently returned, with Tracey's hand in his and Mrs Ward beside him. Katrina went to meet them and the professor said, 'Katrina, this is Mrs Ward,' and, when they had shaken hands, 'and Tracey...'

She was small for her age, with huge blue eyes in a small pale face. She was wearing a cotton mob cap and a cotton dress, very clean but too large. She offered a hand and smiled at Katrina.

Katrina beamed back. 'My goodness, we're going to have fun,' she declared. 'Come in, there's coffee and lemonade.' She glanced at the professor. 'You'll have a cup of coffee before you go back?'

'Please. I'll get the cases.'

Katrina ushered the pair into the cottage. 'I'm so glad to have company,' she told Mrs Ward, 'and I do hope you'll be happy here.'

She led the way into the kitchen. 'Come and sit down; the professor won't be long. Did you enjoy the drive down?'

Mrs Ward was looking uncertain. 'You're sure you don't mind having us? The professor said...'

Katrina gave her a warm smile. 'I'm delighted to have you, and for a start I'm not going to call you Mrs Ward. I'm Katrina...'

'Molly.' Mrs Ward smiled then, and looked around. 'It's like a dream...'

The professor came in, and Katrina poured the coffee, and a glass of lemonade for Tracey, and cut the farmhouse cake she had baked. It was warm from the oven, stuffed with currants and sultanas, and the professor devoured his like a hungry schoolboy and had a second slice, so that Tracey and her mother followed suit. He had two mugs of coffee too, talking easily about this and that, apparently in no hurry to leave, teasing Tracey gently and asking Katrina about the garden. But presently he said, 'I must go back. Mrs Ward, I'll be down in a few weeks to give Tracey a check-up. Katrina knows all about her, and there is an excellent doctor in the village who is a friend of hers.'

He shook hands with them both, nodded at Katrina, and went to the door. 'Phone me at my rooms or in the hospital if you need me, Katrina.'

They all went to the car with him, and on the way he turned aside to look at the moss rose. At the car he said quietly to Katrina, 'Your aunt would have been pleased...'

She understood him. 'Yes, I think so too.' She stared up into his quiet face and marvelled at the thought that she had ever disliked him.

He stared back, smiled suddenly and said, 'Well, well,' in a thoughtful voice. But when he spoke again he sounded exactly like the family doctor. 'I'll expect a weekly report from you, Katrina.'

He got into his car, waved, and was gone.

Katrina led the way back into the cottage. 'Shall we go round the place first? It's a small house and you're welcome to go wherever you want to. There's a big garden too; we'll look at that later. Here's the living room—' she opened the staircase door '—and upstairs...'

They followed her round and Molly said, 'It's beautiful, and so pretty, and all the flowers... No one banging doors or shouting or throwing things.'

'No, it's very quiet here, but the village is only a short walk away. You won't find it strange?'

Mrs Ward drew a contented breath. 'It's heaven,' she said simply. And as for Tracey, darting here, there and everywhere, there was no doubt that she agreed with her mother.

Katrina left them to unpack and went to get lunch on the table. They would have their main meal at one o'clock, she had decided and a substantial tea about five o'clock. She supposed that Tracey would go to bed fairly early, and she could have milk and biscuits at bedtime. Over their meal she asked Molly if she would like this and she agreed readily. 'We've been going to bed quite early together; Tracey was a bit nervous... But here in this dear little house she won't mind going to bed before me, will you, love?'

Tracey had seen Betsy, who had prudently disappeared at their arrival.

'A cat—he's yours? May I stroke him?'

'Of course you may, and he's a she. Betsy. If your mother doesn't mind I dare say she'll pop upstairs when you go to bed, to have a nap and keep you company.'

'She will? Oh, look, she likes me...'

They went round the garden presently, picking

some strawberries for tea and deciding between
beans and peas for tomorrow's dinner.

Molly said, 'You do all this yourself? Grow all
these things?'

'Well, yes. It's a very old garden, and things more
or less grow themselves. I potter most days.' When
Tracey slipped a hand in hers Katrina said, 'We'll all
go and fetch eggs tomorrow, and when you would
like to we'll go to the village. I'm going to take you
to see Dr Peters—just a friendly visit—and the vicar.
There's a village shop, and a post office. Everyone's
very friendly.'

Indoors again, they sat for a while talking idly.
Tracey had taken off her mob cap, and Katrina
winced at the sight of the small bald head, the consequence of chemotherapy.

'She had curls,' said Mrs Ward sadly.

'And will have again,' said Katrina robustly. 'Her
hair will grow once her treatment is completed, and,
what's more, she'll be well.'

'Yes. I can never thank the doctors and nurses
enough, and the professor. He's been so good to
Tracey and the other children he's treating. They
love him; he makes everything fun and he never hur-
ries. I mean, you never feel that he's getting impatient if you don't quite understand...'

She smiled rather shyly at Katrina. 'Is he a friend
of yours?'

'Well, he looked after my aunt until she died, and
he was very good to her—and to me. He's a very
kind man. He leads a busy life, too.'

'Oh, yes,' said Mrs Ward eagerly. 'You should see
him at the hospital. And he has huge clinics and patients on the wards, as well as his own private prac-

tice, but he always looks the same—not tired or worried.'

Katrina reflected that the professor had at least one ardent admirer—possibly dozens more, from what she had been saying about him. And it was all true; again she wondered why she had ever disliked him.

After the first few awkward days, Mrs Ward and Tracey slipped without trouble into the gentle routine of life at Rose Cottage. And Katrina, seeing them both gradually relax, discovered that she was almost happy again. Cooking for three was rewarding work, where making a meal for one had been merely something which had to be done each day, and at breakfast each morning there were plans as to how the day was to be spent...

To Tracey, going to the farm to fetch eggs was a treat; there was a cat with kittens there, and a pet lamb... And Mrs Ward got a tinge of colour into her cheeks and shed a few years. She was a quiet little woman, but quick and intelligent, sharing the household chores and after a while helping Katrina in the garden. They had always lived in London, in a small house in Stepney where her husband had worked. When he'd become ill she had gone out to work while he stayed at home with Tracey, but there had never been enough money. The housing people had moved them into the flat and he had died there.

Such a sad little story, and told with quiet dignity, not asking for pity.

'The professor told me that he thought he could get me rehoused, because of Tracey...'

'Well, if he said that I'm sure he'll do something about it,' Katrina had said. 'Now, we're going to see Dr Peters this morning. You'll like him.'

She'd already taken them to the village shop, and Mrs Dyer, given an expurgated version of the reasons for their visit, duly passed it on to everyone else, so that now Tracey and her mother were greeted by everyone they met. Mrs Ward, used to being ignored or shouted at when she ventured out of their flat, had found this a bit alarming at first, and then delightful.

'Just fancy,' she'd told Katrina, 'they stop and talk—ever so friendly too, and a nice old lady gave Tracey an apple.'

At the end of the week Katrina wrote her report to the professor. And very businesslike it was too. Unaware that he'd phoned Dr Peters, she noted the smallest details in a dry-as-dust way which made him smile. He must find time to drive down and see things for himself...

He was telling his registrar about Tracey one morning when Maureen joined them, listened silently for a moment, and then asked, 'That little girl who had chemotherapy? She's gone to live in the village where my aunt lives? With that big girl I talked to at the fête? Oh, Professor, could you not give her the check-up you want to next weekend? I'm free, and I planned to stay with my aunt. Would you give me a lift? I would be so grateful. I'm not on duty until Monday afternoon, so I can get a train or persuade my aunt to have me driven back.' She gave him a beseeching look. 'I'll be ready at any time you like...'

The professor, thinking about Katrina, said hastily, 'Yes, yes, why not? Be at the entrance at eight o'clock on Saturday morning.' He gave her an absent-minded nod and then turned back to his registrar.

'Now, Tom, about Mrs Turner—she's not taking kindly to chemotherapy...' And Maureen, seeing that he had already forgotten her, slipped away. It had been too good an opportunity to miss.

The registrar watched her go; he said nothing, but he hoped that the professor wasn't going to fall for her—a calculating minx if ever there was one. And his boss was a prize any girl would be glad to win...

The professor laid his plans carefully; Peach was consulted, as was Mrs Peach, and he left his house on Friday evening to spend the night at his flat over his rooms and deal with any last-minute matters at the hospital. He was at the entrance at exactly eight o'clock on Saturday, and Maureen was waiting for him. She wished him good morning, got into the car and, sensing his disinterest, made no effort to talk. What was more she concealed her surprise when he left the main road, drove to his home and stopped before its gate.

'You live here?' she asked, carefully casual.

'Yes, I'm taking the dogs with me.'

A moment later Peach appeared, with a large basket and Barker and Jones. Peach didn't waste time, but stowed the basket in the boot, opened the door for the dogs and stood back with a nod to the professor. Not a moment had been wasted, but he had time to take a good look at Maureen.

'And she spells trouble, mark my words,' he told Mrs Peach.

Almost at the end of their journey, with the village in sight, Maureen said in the winning voice which usually got her her own way, 'May I come with you to see Tracey? She has been such an interesting case...' Which was a mistake, for he had been treating the child long before Maureen had joined his team.

He said coolly, 'I believe you saw her once; she can't be of all that interest to you.' He was already taking the lane to her aunt's house.

Maureen said quickly, 'You are quite right, Professor. But you'll come in for a cup of coffee? It's still early.'

He had stopped before the Manor House and got out to open her door and get her overnight bag from the boot. 'No, thanks. I hope you have a pleasant weekend.' He handed her bag to the butler, who had come out to meet them. 'We have a busy day before us on Monday.'

He got back into the car and drove away, the two dogs, now that she had gone, crowded round him—Barker leaning over the back of his seat, Jones already sitting beside him. The professor heaved an unconscious sigh of content, and pulled up in front of Dr Peters' surgery.

The older man was waiting for him, brushing aside his apology for calling so early in the day. 'I quite often come over on a Saturday morning, to look through the books and so on. You'll want to hear about Tracey... Come in...

'Excellent progress, I should say,' he said later. 'I've seen her several times; Katrina brings her to the village most days—not to the surgery; we don't want to alarm Mrs Ward—just casual chats in the village, and they've been to tea with Mary. I think you'll be pleased. It was a splendid idea of yours.' He looked at the professor. 'Killed two birds with one stone,' he added.

They stared at each other, and the professor smiled. 'Just so. I thought we might have a picnic...'

'Excellent, and such a glorious day too. Katrina is enjoying having them...'

The professor nodded. 'Good. Shall we go on as we are? It's early days to know if she's out of the woods, but I'm hopeful. And I've got on to the housing people; they need a place where they can live without worries.'

They shook hands, and he got back into his car and drove to Rose Cottage.

The door was open, and someone was singing indoors, and Tracey was bent double over a flowerbed, picking a nosegay. She turned round when she heard the car, and rushed to the gate. She was a shy child, and timid, but over the months she had come to regard him as an old friend. 'Have you come to see me? Don't I look well? Mummy says I'm a little miracle—and do you like my dress? Katrina made it for me, and my cap.'

She tugged at his arm and then drew back a little. 'There's a big dog...'

'He's mine; there's another one in the car too. Don't be afraid, Tracey, they're very gentle.'

He let the dogs out, and after a moment, still clinging to his hand, she stroked first one then the other. Obedient to their master's quiet voice, they offered heads to be scratched and grinned at her before following them soberly up the garden path.

There was no one in the living room, but the sound of hammering from the kitchen. Katrina was standing on a chair, knocking in a nail, while Molly held the chair steady.

'Oh, look who has come!' cried Mrs Ward, and

let go of the chair, a flimsy affair hardly up to bearing Katrina's splendid person.

The professor said, 'Good Morning,' in a general kind of way, and lifted Katrina from her perch. 'Before you fall off,' he explained matter-of-factly. 'I hope I'm not upsetting our plans, but I had the chance of this free day, and it's time I took a look at Tracey.'

Mrs Ward said breathlessly, 'Oh, Professor Glenville, she's so well—just look at her. It's wonderful here...'

He smiled at her and looked at Katrina, rather pink and untidy and taking care not to look at him. She felt suddenly shy, which was absurd, and she needed a minute or two to regain her normal calm manner.

Careful to pin her gaze over his shoulder, she said, 'You're not upsetting any plans, Professor, and Tracey—that is—we're all pleased to see you. I'll make us some coffee.'

Tracey came and took her hand. 'There's two dogs. Do you suppose Betsy will mind?'

'No, love, I'm sure she won't. Why don't you take the professor and Mummy into the garden, and I'll call you when the coffee is ready?'

'An excellent idea,' said the professor, and smiled to himself. Katrina hadn't had the time to get behind her normally cool manner, and the flustered girl he saw pleased him mightily.

The moment they had gone Katrina rushed up to her room and combed her hair, bitterly regretting that she hadn't bothered to pin it up but had tied it back with a ribbon. But there was no time to do anything about that—besides, if she did he might think that she was doing it for him... She flung powder on her nose and tore downstairs again. By the time the coffee was ready and they were at the door she was, to all intents and purposes, looking her usual rather reserved self. Except for the hair, of course.

The professor, coming into the kitchen, saw that with a small sigh of satisfaction.

They had their coffee in the garden. Tracey, over her timidity with the dogs, was tossing a ball for them.

'She's better, isn't she, Professor?' asked Mrs Ward anxiously. 'She eats for two, and sleeps at nights.' She looked at Katrina. 'And all due to Katrina—such lovely food, and playing in the garden and going for little walks...'

The professor stretched out at his ease. 'Yes, I see a great improvement. I'll have a look at her presently, and I shall want you to come up to St Aldrick's in a week or two for some more tests.'

He sounded so reassuring that Mrs Ward said happily, 'Yes, of course. She won't mind a bit because we'll be coming back here.'

He showed no desire to go, and presently Katrina asked, 'Would you like to stay for lunch, Professor?' She sounded like a polite hostess who wasn't keen on having guests, and he smiled a little.

'Thank you. But may I in turn invite all of you to a picnic? My good Mrs Peach packed sandwiches, and I thought that Tracey might like a day out. There's a kind of open park called Heaven's Gate only a few miles from here—you will know of it, Katrina?' And when she nodded, he added, 'I should be delighted to have your company.'

Tracey had been listening. 'Oh, please may we go—and may Jones and Barker come with us? And may we go now?' The small child's face under the mob cap was very appealing.

'If Katrina agrees?'

The three of them looked at her: Tracey imploringly, Mrs. Ward doubtfully. 'It was only a cold meal...I mean there is nothing to spoil, is there? We could eat it tomorrow.'

The professor said nothing at all. Katrina peeped at his impassive face. 'It sounds marvellous. Of course we'd love to come with you, Professor. Such a lovely day too, and Heaven's Gate is a beauty spot.' She stopped, aware that she was babbling.

He was watching her, careful not to smile. 'Good. Now, if I might give Tracey a quick examination. Upstairs, perhaps?'

While they were away, Katrina cleared the coffee cups and went up to her room. She could hear Molly and Tracey and the professor's quiet voice in the other bedroom; she would have time to do her hair...

Once they were all downstairs again, the professor expressed satisfaction with Tracey's progress. 'I'll get my secretary to let you know which day to come to London,' he told Mrs Ward. 'Perhaps you had better come with them, Katrina.'

She agreed, in a matter-of-fact manner, hiding pleasure at the prospect. She probably wouldn't see him, but he would be there, she reflected in a muddled way.

Heaven's Gate was beautiful; there were other picnic parties there but they found a quiet spot, shaded by trees and with a magnificent view. The professor, much hindered by Tracey and the dogs, carried the picnic basket from the car, and Katrina and Molly unpacked it. Mrs Peach had surpassed herself: little rolls stuffed with cream cheese, ham and smoked salmon, chicken legs and tiny pork pies, salad, potato straws, little pots of fruit jellies and chocolate mousse...

Molly stared in wonder. 'Look,' she whispered to Katrina. 'There's knives and forks and pepper and salt and glasses and paper serviettes.'

The professor and Tracey had gone to admire the view and take the dogs for a run. When they came back Molly said, 'It's lovely, Professor. I've never seen anything like it—only in those magazines at the dentist's and the hospital.'

He lowered his vast person onto the grass. 'My housekeeper loves making cakes and pies. I hope everyone's hungry; I am.'

He opened a bottle of wine, orangeade for Tracey, and they fell to.

It didn't seem quite real to Katrina. Did famous professors with a comfortable lifestyle and probably hosts of friends make a habit of inviting a patient to a picnic? And such a picnic—more a feast! She wondered why he had done it, worried now that perhaps Tracey wasn't going to get better and that he wanted her to have a treat before... Don't think that, she told herself, and looked up to see his eyes on her.

Molly and Tracey had no doubts. They hadn't been so happy for a very long time. They ate and talked and laughed a lot, and the professor maintained a steady flow of light-hearted conversation. Katrina forgot her vague doubts too, ate her fill, teased Tracey gently and joined in the talk. It was all a bit dreamlike, but she was happy. The professor might have his reasons; she was content to let him carry them out.

Presently they tidied away the remains of their feast and Tracey, drowsy from running around with the dogs, curled up against her mother.

The professor rose to his considerable height. 'Katrina and I will take the dogs for a ramble while you and Tracey rest,' he said, and bent to heave Katrina to her feet. 'They need a run.'

She went with him, willy-nilly. Tracey was already asleep and Mrs Ward nodded her head cheerfully. 'I could sit here all day,' she remarked.

Katrina found herself whisked away, a large compelling hand between her shoulders. She said grumpily, 'But I should have liked to have sat and done nothing.'

They were already walking along a path sloping gently downhill. He stopped and turned her round to face him. 'If that is what you really want, Katrina, we'll go back.' He smiled down at her and she caught her breath.

'Well, a walk would be nice,' she said meekly.

back to London?

# CHAPTER SIX

THEY didn't talk much at first, but presently the professor led the conversation round to life at Rose
Cottage.

'You're quite happy with this arrangement? I
know Mrs Ward and Tracey are, but it is after all
your home and your life which is being disrupted.'

'I'm happy,' she assured him, 'really I am. Molly
is an undemanding companion and a great help in
the house, and Tracey is a darling. Is she better—I
mean really better?'

'I believe so. She has a different type of leukaemia
from your aunt. It is prevalent in children, and if it's
caught in time and treated with radiotherapy and chemotherapy it can be cured. At worst there can be a
remission of years. I sincerely hope that we have
cured Tracey, but no doctor would give a positive
answer to that.'

'But if they have to go back to live in London…?'

'I'm dealing with that problem now.' He looked
down at her and smiled. 'And you, Katrina, let us
talk about you for a moment. Do you have sufficient
money? Obviously they are having the best of everything.'

'I've more than enough. It's a very liberal allowance, isn't it? And of course I don't have to buy salad
or potatoes or fruit at present. There's always some
money over each week. Ought I to write and tell
whoever sends it?'

'No, I think not. There may be some weeks or some special occasion when you might need it. What do you intend to do when Mrs Ward and Tracey go back to London?'

Katrina stopped to look at him. 'They're not going back yet? They've only been here just over three weeks…'

'No, no. Don't get alarmed. Provided that the tests I must do very shortly are satisfactory, I hope you will allow them to stay with you for another month or even longer. But you must understand that as soon as Tracey is well enough it is important that she takes up her normal life—school, joining in with other children. They are both happy here, but if I can arrange for them to move to a quieter district, preferably with a garden, or a park close by, then they can build a life for themselves. Mrs Ward is still young, she may marry again, and Tracey must have the chance to be educated and decide her own future.'

They were walking on, side by side. 'And what about you, Katrina, is it not time that you thought of your own future? You have your whole life ahead of you, you must do something with it.'

'Well, I have thought about it a lot. And I think I know what I want to do. I know the librarian at the public library in Warminster; she and Aunt Thirza were friends and she told me once that if ever I wanted a job it might suit me to train as a librarian. I could work there part-time, just helping out, you know, while I trained. They might even take me without much training. I've got three A levels: English, English Literature and Maths.'

'I see that you've been hiding your light under a

bushel. Why did you not start this training when it was first suggested?'

'Well, Aunt Thirza thought that I should wait a while...' She added sharply, 'I've been very happy...'

He said gently. 'Yes, I know. But it seems a very good idea. You will meet people too, probably marry. You would like that?'

'To marry? Oh, yes. I don't think I'm a career girl. I'd like a home and a husband and children. You said once, when I asked you, that you were considering marrying...'

'So I did. We all have our hopes and dreams, Katrina. Some take longer to achieve than others.'

Which was no answer. Indeed, she reflected, it was a gentle snub. A pity that while she had come to the conclusion that she liked him he had had no such feeling about her. Oh, he was friendly and kind, someone to turn to in trouble, but she sensed that he would be that to anyone.

'We should go back,' she said briskly. 'You'll stay for tea? We could have it in the garden.'

He agreed readily and they walked back, talking of nothing in particular and not hurrying, since the dogs were not to be hastened, darting off in search of invisible rabbits. The day was slipping away, as happy days out of doors do.

Presently they all got into the car and went back to Rose Cottage, and while the professor and Tracey went into the garden to pick strawberries and the first of the raspberries, Katrina and Molly filled a tray with tea things. They carried it outside and set the table near the moss rose with scones and cake and a plate of thinly cut bread and butter, a pot of honey

and another of rhubarb jam. Tracey shared out the
fruit into bowls while the professor fetched the tea-
pot, and they sat down to a leisurely tea.

It was still warm. A golden afternoon, thought
Katrina, and one she would remember; Tracey and
her mother were happy, and the professor appeared
to be enjoying himself. He caught her eye and
smiled, and it seemed to her that it was the smile of
someone who liked her after all. She wanted the day
to go on for ever.

'It's time I went,' said the professor. 'I'm going
out this evening.'

'With a lady?' asked Tracey. 'In a lovely dress?'

'With a lady, yes. But I don't know about the
dress, although I'm sure it will be something beautiful.'

'Like Cinderella?'

'I'm sure of it.' He got to his feet. 'This has been
a lovely day. Thank you, Katrina.'

'Well, you brought the picnic…'

'Picnics need people as well as food!' He shook
Mrs Ward's hand and put a kind hand on Tracey's
thin shoulders, then whistled to the dogs and said,
'Come to the gate with me, Katrina.'

'It was kind of you to come,' she said. 'We had a
lovely day—all that food. Please tell Mrs Peach how
much we enjoyed it. I hope you'll have a pleasant
evening. You'll drive carefully?'

He hid amusement. 'Yes. The A303 is a good fast
road. We got held up once or twice this morning,
though.' And, at her look of enquiry, 'I gave
Maureen Soames a lift; she's spending the weekend
with her aunt.'

Katrina didn't try to understand the feelings of unhappiness which swamped her insides. She said, 'Oh, I see. I expect you're going to pick her up now…'

'No, no. She will be driven back by her aunt's chauffeur.'

Katrina bent to pat first Barker then Jones. 'I hope you have a nice evening,' she repeated, aware that she had said that once, and aware too that her lovely day was spoilt. He need not have told her; on the other hand he might have done so to make it quite clear that even though he'd chosen to spend the day at Rose Cottage it had been for the sole reason of checking up on Tracey.

She watched him get into the car, and nodded and smiled when he gave her a brief wave and then went back slowly to the cottage, where Molly and Tracey were happily reliving their day. 'A day to remember,' Molly told her.

Katrina agreed; her memories wouldn't be happy, though.

The professor, driving back to his home, was thinking about the day too. It had been a success until the very last minute, when Katrina had retired suddenly behind her mask of polite coolness. Not that she had said anything untoward, but he had been quick to know it. Perhaps she was wary of getting too friendly with him. He must slow down, he reflected. When she came to London with Mrs Ward and Tracey he must remember that…

He had a busy week ahead of him and his team were waiting for him when he reached the clinic on Monday morning. He wished them good morning without waste of time, and Maureen, who had meant to ask about his visit to Tracey, saw that it would be advisable to hold her tongue. Instead she worked with a will, and at the end of the clinic went away to the ward to check on a patient.

The professor watched her go. 'She's shaping quite well,' he observed to his registrar. 'Seems interested in her work too.'

His registrar gave a guarded reply. A sure way to win the professor's friendship and esteem was to work hard and care for his patients. Maureen was clever, and she knew that she was attractive. She could turn on the charm too. Once she had got him interested in her work, she would use both to good effect... No good telling the chief that, he thought sourly. He had only to sit back and keep an eye on events.

Mrs Ward had a letter the following week, asking her to attend a clinic at St Aldrick's with Tracey at half past eleven in the morning, four days ahead. She should bring with her an overnight case for Tracey, in case it was found necessary to keep her at the hospital for the night.

'There's something wrong,' said Mrs Ward, in floods of tears. 'Why should she have to stay? They've got all day to examine her...'

Katrina said quickly, 'Look, some tests take a long time. It's far better for her to stay until they're checked than come all the way back here and then have to go up again. You'll stay too, of course, and Tracey's been in the ward several times, hasn't she? Don't worry. If there had been anything to worry about the professor would have told you. You know you can trust him.'

Mrs Ward dried her eyes. 'I'm a fool. Of course you're right. You'll come with us, won't you?'

'Yes, of course, and if you have to stay overnight
I'll come home and have everything ready for when
you get back in the morning. Now, how about you
going to Mrs Dyer's and getting a few things? We
need more bacon and some cheese, and Tracey can
have an ice cream. Perhaps it's best if we don't say
anything to her about staying the night; she might
worry for no reason, for probably it won't be necessary.'

There hadn't been such a glorious summer for
years. Four days later, with Betsy fed and attended
to, they left Rose Cottage early in the morning.
Tracey, in her best frock and little mob cap, was
happy at the idea of seeing the professor again, and
Katrina had put her overnight things into her own
large shoulder bag. So far everything was going to
plan, although she *wasn't* happy at the thought of
perhaps seeing the professor again. It wasn't likely,
she told herself; he would be in his small consulting
room and his patients would be brought to him, and
she would be out of sight in the waiting room. All
the same she put on her prettiest dress.

The waiting room was already crowded when they
got to St Aldrick's, and the clinic was running late.
They would probably have to take a later train back.
They sat discussing where they would go for their
lunch, a treat for Tracey for being a good girl, and
then presently they fell silent; Tracey had a book to
read, Katrina and Mrs Ward watched the people
around them. Slowly the benches cleared, and twice
Maureen Soames walked through the room with a
bundle of notes. She looked very professional as well
as pretty in her white coat. Katrina could understand
that she could attract a man with no effort at all.

Presently Tracey was called, and Mrs Ward with her, leaving Katrina to sit idly glancing through a newspaper someone had left behind. It was over-warm and she felt drowsy. But she was roused presently by Molly.

'Tracey has to stay the night. The professor says there's nothing to be worried about, but he wants to see the results of these tests before she goes home. I'm to stay here too. You will go back to Rose Cottage?' She blinked back tears. 'Oh, Katrina, I do hope everything will be all right.'

'If it hadn't been, the professor would have told you, Molly. You can trust him, you know that.' She opened her purse. 'Here are your return tickets, and you may need some more money. Tell Tracey that we'll go to Mrs Dyer's and buy the biggest ice cream she's got tomorrow. Here's the bag—how sensible of you to have packed it. Can I do anything for you before I go?'

Mrs Ward shook her head.

'You have Dr Peters' phone number; ring him if you need help. And good luck.' She kissed Molly's cheek and watched her hurry away before getting up and leaving the waiting room.

She was too late for the train they had planned to catch, so she took a bus to a shopping centre nearby, and had a bun and coffee, and went in search of a gift for Tracey. She soon found what she wanted in a poky little jeweller's shop—a charm bracelet. It wasn't silver, but it was pretty, the kind of thing a little girl would like to wear. She went to catch a bus to the station for the Warminster train which got in a few minutes before the bus for the village left.

Rose Cottage looked peaceful in the late afternoon

sun, and Betsy was waiting for her. She got herself
a meal, fed the little cat and went to bed early. She
didn't think that Tracey and her mother would get
back much before midday, but she would get up early
and have everything ready for them. She'd thought
about them during the evening; she'd thought about
Maureen and she'd thought about the professor, wondering what he was doing with his evening.

He was still at the hospital; it was almost midnight
by the time he let himself into his home.

Another lovely day dawned, with a gentle early-
morning breeze. Katrina had breakfast, tidied the cottage, and set about getting a special lunch. Bacon
and egg pie—Tracey's favourite dish—with peas and
beans and baby carrots. There were still strawberries,
and although the boy who brought the milk had no
cream, he left her extra milk; she made a custard and
grated nutmeg on the top, and left it in the old-
fashioned larder in the kitchen. She made a cake too,
and a batch of scones. Once they were back she
would cycle down to the village and get the ice
cream. She made lemonade too—not out of a packet
or a bottle but using lemons, just as Aunt Thirza
would have done. She set the jug and glasses on the
kitchen table with a plate of cheese straws and a bowl
of roses, offering a welcome when they should return.

She hadn't bothered to pin up her hair, it was just
tied back with a ribbon from her unpowdered face,
and since she had been cooking she had a blue and
white checked apron over her cotton dress. She wondered briefly if there was time to do her hair and

face, but a glance at the clock decided her against it. If they had caught the earlier morning train and taken a taxi from Warminster they would arrive at any minute.

Which they did: Tracey, her mother and the professor.

'We're back,' cried Tracey, skipping into the kitchen to fling herself at Katrina. 'We came in the professor's car, and I'm every bit as well as the next little girl. He told me so!'

Katrina bent to hug her, smiled at Molly and wished the professor a polite good morning. It was vexing the way he always appeared when she wasn't looking her best. She stopped herself just in time from putting her hand up to her hair.

'You'll stay for coffee?' she asked him.

'Yes, please. May the dogs come into the garden?'

'Of course. I'll get them some water and take the coffee into the garden.'

There was a cheerful bustle for a few minutes, but presently they were sitting by the moss rose bush, with the dogs wandering to and fro and Tracey, so happy to be back, off down the garden to look for raspberries.

The professor stretched his long legs. 'Tracey is doing well,' he told Katrina, and smiled at Mrs Ward. 'We must start thinking about finding you somewhere to live. Somewhere there is a good school and a park, even a small garden. But another few weeks here first, if Katrina is agreeable?'

'Oh, yes, for as long as you wish.'

'We shall hate to leave here,' said Molly. 'But if Tracey is going to get quite well, and we can rent somewhere nice and quiet...'

'Something always turns up,' said the professor comfortably. 'May I stay for lunch?'

Katrina said promptly, 'Yes, of course. It's only bacon and egg pie, and strawberries and custard and bread and cheese. I promised Tracy ice cream so you won't mind if I just bike down to Mrs Dyer's and fetch it...?'

'I'll take you in the car while Mrs Ward and Tracey settle in.'

'Settle in?'

He ignored her question. 'Better still, it's such a lovely day we will walk. I could do with the exercise.' He looked Katrina up and down. 'We big people tend to put on weight.'

Katrina choked and Mrs Ward laughed. 'Don't tease Katrina, Professor Glenville. She's perfect as she is.'

He laughed, got to his feet, took the coffee tray back to the kitchen and pronounced himself ready to walk to the village.

'I'm sure it would do you more good to rest quietly in the garden,' said Katrina pettishly.

He said mildly, 'I'm thirty-nine years old, Katrina. Getting on a bit but not yet reconciled to a chair in the garden. Do you consider me old?'

She pulled at the long grasses fringing the road. 'No—no, of course not. Not even middle-aged. But I thought that you might be tired.'

She glanced sideways at him and added hastily because of the look on his face, which she couldn't quite understand, 'Is Tracey really cured?'

'No, but I believe we've managed to reach a state of remission which I hope will last for many years. Mrs Ward understands that, but there is no reason for Tracey to know. She will probably live to a reasonable age, and I hope, happily.

'She's a dear child, and Molly is very brave. I hope to have them settled in a ground-floor flat fairly soon, with a tiny garden—a converted Victorian villa-type. A very quiet street and a school close by. Mrs Ward should be able to find some kind of work if she would like that.'

'You've been very good to them.'

'I know a great many useful people. Why were you upset when I left the other afternoon?'

She hadn't expected that. 'Me? Upset? Why should I be upset?'

'I don't know,' he said mildly, 'that's why I'm asking you.' And when she didn't answer he said, 'Never mind—you don't intend to tell me, do you?' They walked on silently until he asked, 'Do you ever go to Stourhead?'

'Oh, yes. At least, I haven't been for ages, but Aunt Thirza and I went several times. It's beautiful.'

'I've tickets for an evening concert there: music and singing and picnicking on the lawns. Next Saturday. Will you come?'

'Oh, I'd love to. With Molly and Tracey?'

'No. Just the two of us. I'll come for you about half past seven and bring some food with me.'

'Oh, well. That would be very nice. Is it a dressy affair?'

'Something pretty, and a warm wrap in case it gets chilly.'

'Then thank you; I'll come with you with pleasure.' She smiled up at him. 'Here's Mrs Dyer's shop.'

They carried back the cartons of ice cream

wrapped in newspaper, Katrina having avoided Mrs Dyer's interested eye. Heaven knew what tale would be going round the village in the morning. She didn't care, her head full of the delights of Stourhead.

Every crumb of her carefully prepared lunch was eaten, so was most of the ice cream, and when they had finished the professor volunteered to wash up. Since Mrs Ward said that she had promised Tracey that they would go to the farm and fetch the eggs, Katrina felt constrained to dry the dishes.

'You shouldn't be doing this; there is no need, you know.'

'Ah, but there is; I must practise…!'

'Practise? Why?'

'I'm told by my married friends that when the daily help isn't there they are expected to wash the dishes. I'm putting in some practice, as I said.'

She dried a plate carefully. 'You're getting married?'

He said easily, 'It's about time, isn't it?'

She said tartly, 'Well, there was nothing to stop you marrying whenever you wanted to.'

'There is the question of finding the right wife.'

'But now you've found her?' Katrina went on briskly, 'Then you mustn't waste time.' She paused, then allowed her tongue to utter her thought. 'Do I know her?'

'Oh, yes. May I stay to tea?'

A snub, and not even a gentle one. 'I'm sure we shall all be pleased if you stay,' said Katrina primly.

He was in no hurry to go; he sat for a while after they had had their tea and got to his feet reluctantly.

'It will be a pleasant drive back to your home,' said Katrina, leading him briskly out to his car, not wanting him to go but on the other hand longing to see the back of him. He unsettled her.

At the car he paused. 'Thank you for lunch and tea. A pleasant interlude. Mind you're ready on Saturday.'

He bent and kissed her cheek, got into the car and drove off, Jones beside him, Barker lounging on the back seat. She watched the tail-lights disappear and wondered what he was going to do with his evening.

Although she told herself that it was only an evening out, and nothing to get excited about, Katrina spent Saturday peering up at the blue sky, afraid that at any moment it would pour with rain. She had performed her usual morning chores in the quickest time possible, arranged for Tracey and her mother's suppers, done some quick shopping and then retired to her room to do her nails, wash her hair and inspect her dress for any imperfections.

He had said 'something pretty', and she had rooted around in her wardrobe and found a pretty rose-patterned frock, worn to a friend's wedding two or three years ago. It had a long wide skirt and a neat little short-sleeved bodice. After searching drawers she found a pale mohair stole which had belonged to Aunt Thirza. Not the height of fashion, but it would pass muster in a crowd, and besides, it would be dusk for a good deal of the evening.

Tracey thought that she looked beautiful, and Mrs Ward said, 'Oh, Katrina, you're so pretty. Everyone will look at you...'

Katrina, not a conceited girl, thought that unlikely, but she hoped that the professor might at least approve of the dress.

He came punctually, knocking politely on the door before coming in.

He bade everyone good evening, observed that it was exactly the weather for an outdoor occasion and added, 'Very nice, Katrina. Are you ready?'

Tracey tugged his hand. 'Doesn't she look beautiful?' she wanted to know. And added, 'It's not a new dress, but it's pretty, isn't it? And she's washed her hair.'

Mrs Ward said quickly, 'Oh, Tracey, be quiet dear,' and Katrina wished that the ground beneath her feet would open and swallow her up.'

'It is a charming dress,' said the professor seriously. 'Katrina looks like Cinderella.'

Tracey agreed. 'Yes, yes, she does. Only there isn't a Prince Charming...'

'Did you leave Barker and Jones at home?' said Katrina in a high voice.

'Yes. I don't fancy they would enjoy the music, and they are tired. We went for a long walk and found a racing pigeon with a damaged wing. I'll tell you about it some time.'

'You took him home?'

He smiled down at the eager little face. 'Of course. He's wearing a splint and when he's well he'll go home again.'

In the car he kept up a steady flow of gentle talk so that Katrina began to enjoy herself. It had been silly of her to have felt so shy because he had been joking about Cinderella.

It was a short drive, around twenty miles, and the professor didn't hurry. He parked the car and they joined the stream of people making their way onto the grass stretch bordering the lake.

It was very beautiful there, and they found a quiet spot from where they could see the Pantheon at the far end, framed by the giant trees. There were ducks and swans on the lake, and fish easily seen if one walked to the iron bridge by the Pantheon. People threw pennies into the water, presumably for luck. It took the best part of an hour to walk right round the lake, but if one stopped to inspect the grotto and the temple of Apollo and linger among the trees it took twice as long. Katrina thought how much she would enjoy walking its paths with the professor.

He had the picnic basket with him and spread a rug for her to sit on. He said, 'Each time I come here I tell myself that I must come more often.'

'Yes, I know. We came once, Aunt Thirza and I, in the winter. We were about the only people here and there was a heavy frost. It was out of this world.'

He had stretched out beside her, offering her the programme. 'Mostly Mozart and madrigals, and some Delius.'

The concert began and they sat quietly, finding no need to talk. The interval was the signal for the audience to open their picnic baskets, to stroll to and fro and greet friends. The professor spread their picnic on the grass between them: smoked salmon between paper-thin brown bread and butter, tiny pancakes filled with chopped chicken, cheese and crackers, dishes of salad and little pots of creamy custard, chocolate soufflés and trifles. There was white wine in a cooler, and a Thermos of coffee, and even a dish of after-dinner mints.

When the music started again they sat quietly, not talking, sitting side by side, his arm around her shoulders. It was quite dark when the concert ended,

with a starry sky and a bright moon, and the audience
slowly packed up and went to their cars. Theirs was
one of the last to leave, and the car park by the
Spread Eagle pub was almost empty. Neither of them
noticed Lady Truscott's car. Nor did they see
Maureen Soames, sitting in it with her aunt.

It was midnight by the time they reached Rose
Cottage. In the car, on the point of getting out,
Katrina said, 'It was a lovely evening, thank you.
And the picnic—dear Mrs Peach…' She glanced at
his profile. 'I expect you're free tomorrow? You'll
be very late home.'

He didn't answer her but got out of the car and
opened her door.

'I always think that a cup of tea is the ideal way
to end a pleasant evening.'

'You'd like that?' She skipped out of the car,
happy that the evening wasn't to end for a little
longer. She was enjoying his company; more, she
was happy with him. All her small doubts and problems seemed to disappear when he was with her.
They went quietly indoors and found Betsy asleep in
her basket and the table laid for breakfast. He put
the kettle on while she got mugs and milk and sugar.

'That was a delicious cake we had at tea the other
day,' said the professor, and when she fetched it ate
a huge slice.

He got up to go presently, unhurriedly. And when
she would have gone down the path with him to the
car said, 'No, stay here and lock the door after me.'
He stood looking down at her. 'Enjoy your day tomorrow,' he said, and Katrina, filled with a vague
hope of what he might have said, was disappointed.

She said rather stiffly, 'I hope you don't have too busy a week. And thank you again, Professor.'

'Simon,' he said, and bent and kissed her. Not a goodnight peck, not a polite social salute, but a kiss to send her insides aglow.

This will not do, said Katrina to herself, tumbling into bed. He's going to get married. We don't even know each other well.

All the same she woke in a glow of happiness in the morning, although she didn't allow her thoughts to dwell on the previous evening. She gave a faithful description of the gala at Stourhead to Tracey and Molly, described what dresses she had noticed, praised the concert and detailed the contents of the picnic basket.

'It sounds very nice,' said Molly. 'You should go out more often. I hope us being here doesn't stop you from that.'

She looked so anxious that Katrina said at once, 'Of course it doesn't. I have never gone out a great deal—only in the village, tennis parties and so on. Aunt Thirza and I led very quiet lives. Who is coming to church?'

It was as they left church that she came face to face with Maureen. She would have walked on after a civil good morning, but Maureen laid a hand on her arm.

'Wasn't the concert at Stourhead simply splendid?' she asked. 'I loved every minute of it. I'm so glad that Simon thought of taking you—he was a bit disappointed when I told him I'd already arranged to go with a party from the Manor. Such a pity, for we both share a love for good music. At least Mrs Peach's picnic wasn't wasted...'

Katrina said evenly, 'She makes splendid meals, doesn't she? It was a delightful evening, and so fortunate that it was such a fine night. You're here for the weekend?'

'Yes, I'm to be collected this evening. So silly, really. If I'd known that Simon was free I could have cancelled lunch with friends today. Still, there is still this evening.'

Katrina said quietly, 'Yes. You'll be hard at work again on Monday, I expect.'

Maureen's smile made her grit her teeth. 'Oh, yes, but it isn't all work, you know.' She glanced round her. 'I don't know how you can bear to live here in this dump. I suppose if you've never lived anywhere else you get resigned to it.'

'Never resigned,' said Katrina slowly. 'You see, we have time to live here. I must go. Tracey will be wanting her dinner.'

'Oh, that child Simon talks about. I must say she looks ridiculous in that silly cap.'

Katrina said suddenly, 'You know, I find it hard to believe that you're a doctor. Goodbye.'

She raged silently all the way home to Rose Cottage, answering Mrs Ward's gentle chatter mechanically. How could the professor love, even like such a horrible woman? And why couldn't he have been honest and told her why he had invited her to Stourhead? She wouldn't have minded.

Yes, she would, she had to admit. But never again, she told herself. No more outings with him. If he came again she would find some excuse for being out of the house. Molly could give him a meal if he wanted, and the only reason he would come would be to see Tracey.

'I wish the professor would come to tea,' said Tracey as they ate their lunch. 'Do you suppose he might?'

'No,' said Katrina firmly, 'it's most unlikely. He has lots of friends, and it's only when he comes to see how you are that he stays for tea. Now that you are so well he won't need to come so often, will he?'

'Will I go to see him in hospital again?'

'Of course.' Katrina glanced at Molly. 'But you and Mummy know the way now; you can go together and perhaps you will see him for a little while—just enough time to tell him about the garden and the chicks at the farm.'

She spoke cheerfully, and Mrs Ward backed her up. 'How about taking some eggs for him next time we go? He'll love one with his tea, just like you do.'

They went for a walk in the afternoon, and spent the rest of the day in the garden, reading and chatting idly, and then playing Snakes and Ladders with Tracey.

Monday was another day, thought Katrina, getting ready for bed. The beginning of another week. She allowed her thoughts to dwell on the professor, wondering what he was doing. Possibly driving Maureen back to London.

She got into bed and closed her eyes, only to find his face mirrored on their lids. 'This is ridiculous,' said Katrina aloud, and at length went to sleep.

# CHAPTER SEVEN

THE professor had made it plain that Mrs Ward and Tracey would be returning to London within the next few weeks. A month to six weeks, Katrina thought. It all depended on a suitable home being found for them. But it had been a warning to her that she must consider her future once more.

Leaving Mrs Ward and Tracey to do the shopping, she went along to the library in Warminster. Her luck was in; the head librarian hadn't forgotten her, and what was more told her that within the next month or so there would be a vacancy for a part-time helper in the library. Three days a week, and although the money wasn't much she would be able to manage; it was a foot in the door, thought Katrina, and she could study for exams and in time become a librarian. She told herself that she was a lucky girl and went to find Molly and Tracey.

They had ices in a small café in the High Street, and then went round Woolworth's so that Tracey could spend her pocket money. Mrs Ward bought wool and knitting needles; Tracey would need woollies for the winter.

She said, half apologetically to Katrina, 'I must start thinking about when we go back to London.'

'Well, of course you must. I shall miss you both very much, but it will be rather exciting moving into a new home, and Tracey will like going back to school.'

'You will come and see us?'

'I'd love to.'

Two weeks later, obedient to a letter from the Professor's secretary, Tracey and her mother went to London once more. Katrina stayed at home and paid some long-delayed visits around the village to various friends.

She had tea with Dr Peters and his wife, and told them a little of her future plans.

'It does sound very nice, dear,' said Mrs Peters. 'A bit dull, but I expect you'll meet some nice young people—I mean, so many people go to the library, don't they? You'll miss your visitors.'

Katrina agreed. 'Yes, I shall, but it's marvellous that Tracey is well enough to lead a normal life.'

Dr Peters said, 'Glenville is a good man, has a good deal of success with his patients. He's kept busy, what with his own practice and the travelling round he does to various hospitals. We were at the Manor the other evening, and Lady Truscott was telling us that her niece—remember her, Katrina?—is very happy working in his team. They're good friends. Indeed Lady Truscott hinted that they were slightly more than that. I must say she's a very attractive girl.'

He took a bite of cake. 'Time he got married anyway.'

Katrina said brightly, 'They must have a great deal in common...'

'Not that I like the girl overmuch,' said Mrs Peters surprisingly. 'No warmth, if you know what I mean. She'll make a most suitable wife and spend his money, but that won't be of much use to him, will it? He needs a loving wife.'

Dr Peters laughed. 'Like you, my dear?'

'Like me.'

Like me, thought Katrina. The sudden clear thought emptied her head of anything else. And how strange to be so sure of something so completely alien to her previous feelings about the professor. When, she wondered, had her vague dislike of him changed to love, and why hadn't she known about it? And now she did know about it, and a lot of use that was!

Alone that evening she sat down and thought about it. She felt excited, but sad too, for nothing would come of her love. She would have to steel herself to hearing of his engagement to Maureen. 'What a good thing that I have a career as a librarian before me,' she told Betsy.

She woke in the night and wondered if he would bring Tracey and Mrs Ward back, for Tracey was spending the night at the hospital again. She longed to see him again, but she must remember to be cool—friendly, but cool. It would be hard...

She got up early, and after breakfast set about preparing lunch. She would cook a little more of everything just in case he came. She set the coffee ready and made a batch of biscuits, made sure that her hair was tidy and her face nicely made-up, and then sat down to wait.

The morning had slipped away to early afternoon when Mrs Ward and Tracey came. They had missed the train, they told her, and wasn't it marvellous that Tracey need not have another check-up for three months? And there was a flat they could move into in three weeks' time.

They both talked at once, and Katrina, despite her disappointment, was delighted for them.

'Have you seen it? Where is it?'

'Not yet. The professor's coming to fetch us on Saturday afternoon so that we can see it. Isn't it exciting? And the Social Services are letting me have some furniture, and I've saved quite a bit of money so's we can have curtains and a rug or two.'

Mrs Ward flung her arms round Katrina. 'Oh, Katrina, you don't know how happy I am.'

They spent a delightful hour or so discussing furnishings, and Katrina promised herself that she would make some excuse to leave the cottage on Saturday so that she wouldn't see the professor.

'At what time are you to be fetched?' she asked casually.

'Early in the morning, around nine o'clock, and we're to be ready and not bother about coffee or anything.'

Katrina, always an early riser, got up even earlier than usual on Saturday. It had rained during the night, but the morning was glorious. She got into a cotton dress and sandals, roused Mrs Ward and Tracey, got breakfast and, when they had eaten it, cleared the table.

When they came downstairs, dressed and ready to wait for the professor, she said suddenly, 'Oh, I quite forgot. I must fetch the chicken from the farm. I'll go straight away before it gets too warm. You've a key, haven't you, Molly? If I'm not back before you go, lock the door, will you? Have a lovely day, and remember to tell me everything when you get back.' She added in a suitably casual voice, 'I promised I'd go and see Mrs Peters this afternoon. If I'm not back, give the professor coffee if he would like it.'

She hugged Tracey, got on her bike and pedalled away briskly. It wasn't quite nine o'clock; she would stay until ten o'clock to be on the safe side.

She fetched the chicken and, since she had time on her hands, left her bike in the ditch and climbed a gate into a small field shaded by trees, to sit idly thinking about the professor and her future. But thinking about him was foolish and a waste of time, so she concentrated on the job awaiting her at the library. When she heard the church clock striking ten she got on to her bike and cycled back to Rose Cottage.

The Bentley was parked outside and the professor was leaning over the gate. 'There you are,' he said cheerfully, 'Mrs Ward's making coffee, then we'll be off.' He eyed her dress. 'That's nice; come as you are.'

'I'm not coming,' said Katrina, and hoped he couldn't hear her heart thumping. 'I've a lot to do in the garden, and there's the chicken and Mrs Peters...'

He opened the gate for her. 'Dear girl, we won't go until you say that you will come with us. Tracey will break her heart.'

He was standing much too near her for comfort. 'Yes, well—I dare say she won't mind if I explain.'

'Oh, yes, she will. Pretend I'm not here, ignore me completely if you wish, and when you are in a better temper you can tell me why you avoid me. Now run along and put the chicken away and we'll pour the coffee.'

'My hair...'

'Delightful, but I dare say you want to look severe. Go and pin it up, then. You can have five minutes.'

He smiled at her and she caught her breath, because it was tender and just a little amused, and since she could think of no further argument she did as she was told.

Half an hour later they were on their way. Mrs Ward beside the professor, Katrina and Tracey in the back. Reaching London, the professor drove across the city's heart until he reached Bow. The main street was bustling, and the shops were small and for the most part shabby, but the narrow roads leading from it were lined with well-cared-for houses. Mostly small, but here and there larger Victorian town houses of three or four storeys. Into one of these streets the professor drove, and presently stopped before one such house facing a small fenced plot of grass and small trees.

There was no basement and no front garden, but the door opened onto a room hall with a staircase at one side and a smaller door beside it. He took a key from his pocket and opened it and ushered them in.

There was a tiny hall, with a door at its end and two doors along one wall. The first door opened onto a fair-sized room with a bay window overlooking the street. The wall had been distempered pale yellow and there was a small electric fire in the fireplace.

Mrs Ward looked around her. 'Is it a bed-sitting room?'

'No, no. Come through here.' He led the way through a door in the end wall into a smaller room with a window looking out onto a small garden, and at Tracey's squeal of delight said, 'Yes, the garden is yours too. Come and see the kitchen.'

This was a slip of a room, but nicely fitted with shelves and cupboards. There was a small window here too, and a door leading to the garden. And leading from the kitchen a bathroom, very basic, but there was a gas geyser over the bath and a small washbasin.

Mrs Ward had her arms round Tracey. 'It's not true. I couldn't never afford it even if it was.'

'Come into the garden,' invited the professor, and he opened the kitchen door. It was very small, fenced in and neglected, but Katrina, casting her eyes around it, was already planting it in her mind's eye, and there were several overgrown shrubs and a rose bush or two which only needed a little loving attention...

'Like it?' the professor wanted to know.

'Oh, sir, it's wonderful. Only as I said, it'll cost too much to rent.'

'Well, the Social Services are asking a very reasonable amount, and you will have a grant to buy basic furniture and help towards gas and electricity and so on. There's a good school about five minutes' walk from here.'

'I could get work. I did before, you know—cleaning for ladies.'

'Then would you like to come with me now, and we can settle the matter at once?'

'I'll never be able to thank you enough.'

'Tracey has been such a brave little girl you both deserve a reward, Mrs Ward. Do you want to take another look before we go?'

Katrina stayed in the car while they went to arrange about the flat. They were there a long time and it was warm in the car. She sat thinking about Mrs Ward's happy face and Tracey's excitement.

The professor wasn't just kind; he had gone to a lot of trouble on Mrs Ward's behalf and kept very quiet about it. Katrina had no doubt in her mind that he had helped other patients in a similar manner. There was a great deal she didn't know about him. Had he parents alive, brothers and sisters, and where did they live? He never spoke of himself, and only occasionally of his work, but she had no doubt that he had friends enough.

Mrs Peters, who enjoyed a good gossip, had confided in her one day: Lady Truscott had mentioned in a smug way that he was attracted to Maureen, despite numerous attempts by other equally charming girls to attract his attention. Katrina had no doubt that that was true; he was a prize—successful in his profession, well-off, good-looking, possessing a lovely house. On the other hand she doubted if he found any of these things other than his work important.

She longed to get to know him better. There was no hope that he would fall in love with her, but if she knew more about him at least she would have more to remember him by...

They came back to the car presently, Mrs Ward and Tracey both talking at once, anxious that Katrina should have a share in their delight. When they paused for breath the professor observed quietly that they could discuss the rest in comfort over a meal, and drove back towards the City. On Islington's fringe he parked before a small restaurant in a narrow street.

It was half filled, light and airy, its tables covered in white cloths, with small vases of flowers and immaculate silverware. Exactly right, reflected Katrina, studying the menu. Not so elegant that Molly and

Tracey might have felt out of place, but elegant enough to make the meal a treat to remember.

She and the professor had hardly exchanged a word. Now he asked casually, 'Is there anything special you would like, Katrina? A salad? Salmon fish cakes?'

He glanced at her as he spoke and she said at once, 'Oh, I'd like the fishcakes and some French fries.' She saw Mrs Ward's look of relief as she and Tracey said they would like that too. The fish cakes weren't frozen, they were delicious, and presently the pair of them were joining in the easy talk Katrina and the professor had started, any awkwardness about their surroundings quickly forgotten.

The meal was a great success, made even more so by the pudding trolley loaded with so many delicacies that Tracey couldn't make up her mind until the waiter suggested that she might have a little of several of them.

They didn't hurry over their coffee, and Katrina wondered if the professor was impatient to see them back to Rose Cottage. If he was, he gave no sign.

Katrina wasn't quite sure how she came to be sitting with the professor on their return journey, nor why. It wasn't as though he wanted to talk, for they exchanged barely a word during the whole trip. Perhaps he thought that Mrs Ward and Tracey would like to be together so that they could discuss their future. She sat quietly, watching his hands on the wheel, and tried to think of some intelligent remark to break the silence. And that was a waste for he said quietly, 'No need to talk, Katrina.'

A remark which rendered her dumb.

At Rose Cottage she offered him tea in a voice to

freeze his bones, but he refused cheerfully, bade Mrs
Ward and Tracey goodbye, patted her on the shoulder in a brotherly fashion, observing that they would
probably meet at some time, and then drove off.

Probably a polite way of bidding her goodbye; he
had no need to come again. He had thanked her for
having Tracey and her mother, it had been an arrangement which had suited both of them, and that
was that. Katrina told herself to grow up and stop
behaving like a silly girl instead of a sensible woman,
and threw herself into the preparations for Tracey's
return to London.

The village knew almost at once, of course, and
since there was nothing very much happening for a
week or two great interest was shown in their departure. Mrs Peters, kindness itself, gave a little tea
party for them, and the Mothers' Union handed Mrs
Ward an embroidered tablecloth for her new home
and a doll for Tracey. Molly, bearing her gifts back
to the cottage, cried all over Katrina. 'Everyone's so
kind,' she sobbed, 'and I'm so happy.'

'You've a lot of friends here,' said Katrina brac-
ingly, 'and when you want a holiday you'll always
be very welcome. Shall we go to Warminster tomorrow and see if there are any odd lengths of curtain
material? They have some very smart clothes there
too. Fit yourself out while you have the chance,
Molly.'

So they all went to Warminster and spent a long
time browsing in charity shops. It was a pity they
didn't know the size of the windows, but the dis-
carded curtains, some of them of excellent material,
were so cheap it was worth buying them.

Katrina, examining a length of flowered chintz,

suggested that they went up to Bow and got the measurements and made the curtains up before Mrs Ward left. 'And while we're here, look at this jacket. It's your size, and such a nice colour. It would take you right through the winter too—let's find a skirt…' And before she went back home she bought corduroy velveteen in a pretty blue, enough to make Tracey a dress and matching mob cap.

It was a tedious journey to Bow, but worth it. They left Tracey in Mrs Peters' kind care and spent several hours making lists and measuring. Mrs Ward's bits and pieces of furniture which had been stored were to be augmented by the Social Services—a bed for Tracey, a comfortable chair, a chest of drawers and a dressing table and wardrobe. They went round arranging the furniture in their heads, and spent some time in the little garden.

'I'll come up in the autumn,' said Katrina, 'and bring you bulbs and some rose trees. And I'd love to come up one day once you've settled in and dig the garden over. Then you can plant things as you want to.'

'Will you really? But you said you would have a job?'

'Only part-time…'

The day of their departure arrived. There had been no sign of the professor, no message, nothing. They were to travel by train; there was a midday bus which would take them to Warminster, and Katrina was going with them to see them safely on the train. She had offered to go all the way with them, but Molly had declined. 'You don't mind? You see, we want to be there together, just Tracey and me—you know?

Arranging things and making the beds and having supper. You do understand?'

'Yes, I do, Molly. I'd want to do that if I were you. Only promise me that if you should need help you'll let me know. You had friends before, didn't you? Once they know that you are back in London they'll come and see you.'

They had brought their luggage downstairs, and Katrina was checking that they had everything when there was a knock on the door.

Simon, thought Katrina, forgetting that she must never think of him as that, only as the professor, and flew to the door. Peach stood there.

'Peach—good morning. How nice to see you! Come in…'

She led him into the living room, at a loss for words.

'Good morning, miss. The professor sent me to drive Mrs Ward and her little girl to their flat. He's unable to come himself. The journey might be too tiring for them and they may need a little help when they get there.'

'Peach, how kind. You'll have a cup of coffee? It won't take long and you'll be glad of five minutes' rest.'

She called to Molly and Tracey, and when they came downstairs introduced Peach and left them to get coffee. It was the sort of thoughtful gesture the professor would make, and it would turn a long, tiring journey into a pleasant trip. She warmed the milk and wondered what Simon was doing. Peach had said that he was unable to come—was he ill? On holiday? Or just too busy at the hospital? The thought of him being ill made her feel quite sick, until she reminded herself that he was the kind of man who never got ill.

Presently Peach stowed the luggage in the boot, waiting patiently while Katrina packed eggs and butter, a bottle of milk and half a loaf of bread into a plastic bag. She had the rest of the day in which to replenish her larder…

She said goodbye to Molly, and then hugged Tracey before they got into the car. A nice car, she reflected, a Rover—surely Simon didn't have two cars? She would have liked to have asked Peach but she decided not to.

The cottage was very empty when they had driven away. She went upstairs and collected bed linen and towels and put them into the washing machine, then set about turning the room out. It would be something to do, and since Molly was no longer there to talk to she talked to Betsy. Later she cycled down to the village and phoned the librarian.

A librarian would be going on holiday at the beginning of the week. Katrina could start then, working full time, but then there would be no vacancy for part-time work until the beginning of September.

I'm very lucky, she told herself, cycling back to the cottage to hang out the sheets and then call in at Dr Peters' surgery. He took her back to his home for a late tea and she told him and Mrs Peters of her plans.

'It's so fortunate,' she said brightly, 'and I know I shall enjoy working at the library. Only two weeks for now, but part time in September suits me beautifully.'

That evening she sat down and did her sums. There would be a final cheque for Mrs Ward and

Tracey's board and lodging, but she had saved nothing from the previous payments; anything which had been over she had used to buy extras for Tracey. But there was enough in her purse to see her round until she was paid at the library. Her future, she told herself, was assured. Contemplating it, she sat there, tears rolling down her cheeks.

She felt better in the morning. Wasting time on dreaming of something she could never have was foolish; she could hear Aunt Thirza's voice saying so—so she turned the cottage upside down, spent hours in the garden and told any of her friends who asked her that she was looking forward to working at the library. And actually, when Monday came and she presented herself there, she enjoyed it.

Being a novice, her work was simple enough: sorting books onto the shelves, opening the mail, making the morning coffee and being shown the routine. She knew nothing of computers, but she was intelligent and quick, and by the end of the week she was fitting in very nicely. The head librarian had welcomed her warmly, but at first the other two young women who worked there had viewed her with mild dislike. They were jealous of their positions and suspected her of trying to usurp them, but after a few days they decided to accept her as a fellow worker, enjoying giving her the lowly jobs to do, airing their superior knowledge. Katrina didn't mind; she had a job, she was too tired to be unhappy and the money was a godsend...

She had a letter from Molly, happiness spilling from every page. The flat was perfection, the furniture fitted exactly as she wanted it, the curtains were lovely and she had bought some rugs. Peach had stayed for an hour or more, helping her, and Tracey was over the moon at having a bedroom to herself. Life was just perfect, wrote Molly, and when was Katrina coming to see them?

Work at the library would end after the second week; Katrina wrote that she would come on the Sunday following that. The journey would cost money she might have saved, but she had promised that she would go—besides, she was wanting to see Molly's new home now that it was furnished.

She bade them a temporary goodbye at the library at the end of her second week, and spent Saturday catching up on household chores, necessary shopping and going to fetch eggs to take to Molly. She packed a basket with a trowel, some cuttings from the garden, chocolate for Tracey and the eggs, put everything ready for the morning and went to bed early, glad of Betsy's company.

She was on the point of leaving to catch the bus the next morning, and had just gone upstairs to make sure that the windows were closed, when she looked out and saw the Bentley at the gate and the professor coming unhurriedly up the path.

She flew downstairs to open the door.

'You can't stay,' said Katrina, in a fine flurry. 'I am catching the bus—I'm going to see Molly and Tracey.'

His, 'Good morning, Katrina,' was slightly reproving.

'Oh—good morning…' she added.

'That's better, just for a moment I thought you weren't glad to see me.'

'Well, of course, I'm glad…'

She shouldn't have said that, for he swept a great

arm round her and kissed her. A gentle kiss, given without haste. She would have liked it to go on for ever, but it didn't; he said briskly, 'Are we ready to go?'

'Go? Go where? I shall miss my bus... If you'd run me to the village I'll just have time.'

He had picked up Betsy, making much of her. 'Mrs Ward expects us for lunch. We'll stop at my place for coffee.' He smiled with a great charm and Katrina's heart turned over. 'I have a day off.'

He put the little cat down, picked up the basket and asked, 'Shall we go?'

There was no alternative even if she had wished to take it—and she didn't. She waited meekly while he locked the door, gave her the key and then opened the car door. Barker and Jones were on the back seat, delighted to see her, but they settled down when the professor got into the car and sent the Bentley sliding soundlessly away.

Presently Katrina said in a voice she strove to keep cool, 'This isn't at all what I had planned.'

'Ah, that's life for you.' The professor sounded cheerfully casual. 'One never knows when one's plans are going to be altered. Have you heard from Mrs Ward? She sounded very content.' And at Katrina's enquiring look he added, 'I asked her to phone me when she heard from you.'

'Why?'

'Now that I've found you, Katrina, I don't want to lose sight of you.'

She couldn't think of an answer to that. Something in his voice convinced her that he wasn't joking, but if he wasn't joking what exactly did he mean? But apparently he didn't expect an answer. 'How do you like your work at the library?'

'Very much. I can start again at the beginning of September, and that suits me—there's a lot to do in the garden, and Mrs Dyer will take anything I like to sell her.' She added hastily, in case he should think she was hard up, 'It's a pity to waste it.'

Gardening was a safe topic, and he made no effort to change the subject. Katrina was quite glad when he drew up at his own front door. There was still the drive up to Bow, she reflected, responding to Peach's welcoming smile. What on earth were they to talk about?

They had coffee in the drawing room while the dogs raced round the garden. 'Are they coming with us?' asked Katrina.

'Yes, Tracey wants to see them again. Katrina, will you have dinner with me this evening?' He smiled at her. 'Here—and not too late, for I know you will want to get back to Betsy.'

'Thank you, I'd like that.' She added anxiously, 'I'm not keeping you from anything more important?'

'No, there is nothing more important, Katrina.' He was still smiling, and she looked away because she was blushing and that annoyed her—behaving like a shy schoolgirl...

She need not have worried about making small talk on their way to London; she had discovered that there was no need for that. The silence between them was comfortable, and they broke it from time to time, talking like old friends. She was sorry when London began to close in on them.

The streets were comparatively empty, and the

side-streets outside Mrs Ward's flat were quiet, and
the warmth of their greeting left them in no doubt
that they were both welcome. The basket was unpacked, a bottle of wine from the professor set to
cool and the whole party went on a tour of inspection.

Mrs Ward had turned the little place into a home;
the furniture was cheap, shabby, and nothing
matched, but everything was polished, there were
some pretty cushions and the curtains were a great
success. There were colourful rugs on the floors, and
flowers on the tablecloth the Mothers' Union had
given them, and a pretty lamp by Tracey's bed.

'It's marvellous,' said Katrina. 'You must have
worked hard. It's so cosy, as though you've been
living here for years.'

Molly beamed. 'You really think so? And I've got
a job already—at Tracey's school; they wanted a dinner lady. It's only five minutes' walk away, and I
can make sure that Tracey eats properly. Now come
and have dinner, but we'll have a drink first. It's a
celebration.'

They drank their sherry and the professor, swal-
lowing his with every sign of enjoyment, thanked
heaven that he had brought a bottle of wine with him.
When it was poured, he accepted Mrs Ward's opinion that it tasted very nice—far better than the wine
she had brought from the Co-op—with becoming
modesty.

Katrina, watching him with Tracey, thought what
a splendid man he was; he was at home with everyone, never talking about himself, apparently never
tired. But there was another side to him, she felt sure;
she had glimpsed it once or twice. He liked his own

way and wasn't to be turned from it, and she thought that if his temper was aroused he could be a very angry man. He looked up suddenly and smiled at her, and she smiled back, not minding if her feelings showed.

Molly had taken great pains with the lunch: cold meat and salad, tinned fruit and ice cream, and afterwards she and Katrina washed up while the professor went into the garden with Tracey. By the time the two women had got out there he had grubbed up weeds, cut back the tangle of overgrown shrubs with his pocket knife and dug holes here and there in the narrow flowerbeds for the cuttings Katrina had brought with her. He had the air of a man contented with his lot, and Tracey, picking up stones and putting them into an empty tin, was singing in a small out-of-tune voice.

Molly said softly, 'Oh, he ought to marry and have children of his own.'

Katrina gave the back of his head a look of love, and said, 'Yes, well, I suppose he will one day.' The thought hurt.

They left soon after tea, promising to come again, and as he drove west the professor said, 'You don't know the date of Mrs Ward's birthday, I suppose?'

'Yes, September the fifth.'

'She needs gardening tools. But I can hardly give her a present—may I send them in your name?'

'You mean she's not to know that you've given them to her?' Katrina thought about that. 'Yes, well, I can see what you mean. Yes, all right. Look, if you get her a fork and spade I could give her a rake. And you want me to say that they are all from me?'

'Please. You think that they have settled in?' He glanced at her. 'Tracey seems happy and looks well.'

'Oh, they're happy; they're over the moon. If only Tracey can keep well...'

'We shall do our best. Now, tell me, Katrina, you will be at Rose Cottage until you start work again in September?'

'Oh, yes. Do you want to send another patient to stay with me? I liked having Molly and Tracey.'

'No. I want you to be there, and free, so that whenever I can manage it I can come and see you.'

'See me? Why?'

'I've fallen in love with you, but you don't feel the same about me yet.' When she would have spoken, he said, 'No, don't say anything, just bear it in mind.'

He had spoken in a casual voice, and now added, 'You won't mind if I just turn up from time to time?'

Katrina drew a steadying breath. 'No. I shan't mind.'

# CHAPTER EIGHT

AFTER that they didn't talk much; there was no need, they were content with each other's society. Katrina allowed her thoughts to wander, not trying to see too far into the future but quietly happy. She sensed that Simon wasn't going to say anything more until he was ready, and besides, she clearly remembered Aunt Thirza observing once that it was easy to fall in love and even easier to fall out of it again. All the same, just for the moment, she was happy.

Peach had the door open as they got out of the car. The professor saw her to the door and said, 'I'll take the dogs for a quick run. Peach will show you where you can tidy yourself.'

She was quite tidy. All the same she powdered her nose and tucked back some strands of hair before going to the drawing room. She hadn't hurried and the professor was already there, with the doors to the garden open so that the dogs could go in and out. They came to her as she went in, before racing off with Peach for their supper.

It was still early evening, and they sat by the open door, drinking their sherry, until Peach came to tell them that dinner was served. And over the mushrooms in garlic, the salmon cutlets, the cucumber and orange salad and the profiteroles and whipped cream, they talked about everything under the sun like old friends. Only the professor said nothing about himself, and when she asked, carefully casual, if he was busy at the hospital he told her briefly that he would be away for several days.

She longed to ask more, but something in his voice stopped her. She began to talk about the garden, a safe subject in which they were both interested.

He didn't attempt to delay her when she put down her coffee cup and asked if he minded if she went back to Rose Cottage.

She bade Peach goodbye, thanked Mrs Peach for a delicious dinner and got into the car once more while Barker and Jones scrambled onto the back seat. Katrina, making small talk, found the journey far too short.

At the cottage he got out and opened her gate and walked up the path with her. He took the key from its hiding place, opened the door and stood aside for her to go in. Betsy came to meet her and she stooped to pick her up.

'Thank you for a lovely day,' she said. 'It was wonderful to see Mrs Ward and Tracey so happy.' She added, in case that sounded ungrateful, 'And I enjoyed the drive too.'

He stood looking down at her, smiling a little. He bent and kissed her gently. 'I shall see you soon,' he said 'Sleep well.'

He pushed her gently into the cottage and shut the door, and a moment later drove himself away.

Katrina wandered into the kitchen and put the kettle on; a cup of tea might help her to come down from cloud nine and be her sensible self once more.

There was plenty to keep her busy during the next few days. Now that she was on her own again she went out and about to her friends, meeting them for coffee, playing tennis, giving a helping hand at the bring-and-buy sale at the church school. It was here she met Lady Truscott again.

'So your guests have gone, Katrina.' She gave a tinkling laugh. 'Well, "guests" is not quite the right word, is it? Professor Glenville must have been glad to find someone to take them in until they could be found somewhere suitable to live. Aftercare is so important, so Maureen tells me. He is planning a series of lectures around the country and she has high hopes of going with him.'

'Whatever for?' Katrina asked. 'Is she going to give lectures too?'

Lady Truscott laughed. 'No, no, my dear. As personal assistant—he will need someone.' She smiled archly. 'And I rather suspect as rather more than that.'

Katrina chose to remain obtuse. 'Oh, answering the phone and writing letters?'

'No, no. Maureen is a doctor; she doesn't need to do such things.'

Lady Truscott, who didn't move with the times, had only a vague idea as to the onerous tasks members of the medical profession performed. She laid a hand on Katrina's arm. 'They're very close, you know. Maureen has hinted... Any day now I expect to have delightful news. They will make an ideal couple...' She patted Katrina's arm. 'We must find a nice young man for you, Katrina.'

'No need,' said Katrina. 'I've several up my sleeve. There's Mrs Potter waving; I expect she wants me to help with the teas.'

She gave Lady Truscott a beaming smile and hurried off in a purposeful way. She didn't believe any of Lady Truscott's news. At least, she amended, there might be a grain of truth; he had said he would be away, and probably he did take someone with him when he lectured, but she didn't believe that he and Maureen... Not after last Sunday. He had said, 'I shall see you soon,' and he had kissed her. It hadn't been a peck either. She smiled as she remembered it.

She took some runner beans to Mrs Peters the next morning, and over coffee Mrs Peters observed, 'Lady Truscott seems to think that Maureen and Professor Glenville are going to marry. Did he say anything to you about it?'

Katrina went pink, but she answered in a matter-of-fact manner. 'No, but then he wouldn't, would he? It's nothing to do with me.'

Mrs Peters privately disagreed with that, but she didn't say so, only added, 'Mind you, Lady Truscott is prone to exaggeration.'

But there's no smoke without fire, thought Katrina gloomily.

It was at the end of the week when there was a fire at the Manor. Katrina, picking raspberries in a corner of the garden, caught a whiff of smoke and looked around her. She put down her trug and went to the cottage—she was sure she hadn't left the gas alight on the stove, or the iron on the ironing board, but all the same she went to look.

It was on her way up the garden path that she saw smoke, thin wisps of it, idling across the sky. Not the village, she saw that at once, but to the west of it.

The Manor—a chimney on fire, one of the out-buildings... She flew to get her bike, locked the cottage door and pedalled briskly down the lane. At the edge of the village, where the lane forked into the side-road leading to the Manor, there was no sign of anyone, and she realised that the wind was blowing the smoke away from it. Perhaps it was an extra large bonfire... But, rounding the corner and wheeling into the Manor grounds she could see a lot more smoke now, somewhere at the back of the house. She could hear a few upraised voices too.

She cycled round the side of the house and saw Lady Truscott's portly butler coming from the kitchen door.

She got off her bike and he trotted up to her, very puffed. 'I've phoned the Fire Brigade, miss. That silly girl left a pan on the stove; the kitchen's on fire and she's having hysterics. What's more, Lady Truscott was in her bath—her maid's dressing her.'

Grey smoke curled lazily out of the door behind him and Katrina said, 'Has anyone done anything? Are the doors and windows shut? Can the fire get a hold?'

'I shut the windows...'

'Is there another door? If we go in from the other side,' said Katrina, 'with wet blankets or something like that, we could smother the fire if it's only in the kitchen. Where is everyone?'

'That's the trouble, miss, they're all down at Long Meadow, doing the last of the hay. There's just the girl and myself.'

Katrina leaned her bike against the wall. 'I'll go in through the front. Could you send the girl to Long Meadow and tell the men to come back quickly? The Fire Brigade should be here soon.'

She was walking away as she spoke. Their conversation had been brief, but the fire might take hold unless it was dealt with swiftly. Surely there was a fire appliance in a splendid house such as the Manor…

The front hall was cool and quiet, with only the faintest hint of smoke. She went to the back of the hall and through the baize door which led to the kitchen quarters, cautiously opening doors as she went: still room, pantry, the butler's pantry, laundry room—getting smokier as she went. And when she opened the kitchen door it was to discover the place well alight.

It was frightening: oily smoke and little rivers of flame creeping along the walls. She went back to the laundry room and soaked a towel; she tried to tie it round her face and returned to have another look. The fire was now too big for buckets of water and wet blankets; it had reached the vast dresser, and as she looked a door beside it collapsed under the heat and the flames crept through to wherever was beyond.

Katrina nipped smartly back the way she had come and tried the door on the other side of the staircase. The passage beyond was full of smoke; it must lead to the kitchen too. She shut the door and saw Lady Truscott coming down the staircase. She had clearly dressed in a hurry and was wearing her bedroom slippers.

She hurried over to Katrina. 'They tell me the kitchen's on fire. Why isn't someone putting it out? And I've people coming to dinner this evening. Where is the Fire Brigade? Where is Hysop?'

'He's gone to send the girl to warn the men in Long Meadow. The fire people have been alerted.' Katrina watched smoke oozing under the door. 'Lady

Truscott, I think we should get the smaller furniture and pictures out of the house…and I can't find anything with which I can put the fire out.'

'Oh, one of those canister things? I did have some. Oh, dear, this is most upsetting.' She looked at Katrina. 'Why are you here, Katrina?'

'I saw the smoke. Shall we start on the pictures…?'

'My jewels—the silver! Where is my maid?'

'Probably in your bedroom. If you go and find her I'll start on the dining room silver,' said Katrina, looking uneasily at the smoke, not wisps any more but thick ribbons of dark grey. There was a faint crackling sound too. She hoped that someone, preferably a dozen strong men who would know what to do, would come. In the meantime she must do her best…

Lady Truscott, calling for her maid, went upstairs, and Katrina went into the dining room. There were heavy silver candlesticks, an epergne, hefty silver salvers, and a vast tray on the sideboard. She lugged them out and laid them neatly on the gravel sweep before the house. She knew from previous visits that some of the pictures were valuable, so she carried those out too, and was staggering out of the front door with a hideous ormulu clock when help arrived—the first of the men from the hayfield and at the same time two boys from the village. There were more on the way, they told Katrina, and started carrying out the dainty Regency chairs guests were terrified of sitting on because they were so frail.

Two things happened then: the Fire Brigade arrived and one of the boys fell against the door beside the staircase. It gave way under him and he tumbled through into the smoke-filled passage beyond. By now the place was full of people, and the only person to see him was Katrina. She called to several people around her but there was too much confusion. She dragged a cloth off the table nearby, soaked it in a bucket of water some well-meaning helper had brought with him, and wrapped it round her face. The cloth was one of Lady Truscott's most prized possessions—something to do with the Duke of Wellington, she always told everyone who asked—not that that bothered Katrina. It was wet and it offered some protection.

The boy was sprawled on the floor not far from the door, which was a good thing for the smoke was thinner there. He wasn't unconscious, only dazed and unable for the moment to help himself. Katrina hauled him back into the hall, fetched the bucket of water, propped him against the wall and splashed some of it on to him. There were people milling all around them, and she tugged at trouser legs until a man stopped and looked down.

Katrina got to her feet. 'He fell through the door. He's OK, but could someone look after him?'

'Leave 'im with me, miss. You're OK, are you? Miss Gibbs, ain't it, from Rose Cottage?'

'Yes, I'm fine. I'll go home now; there are more than enough helpers here.'

The professor was sitting in Theatre Sister's office with his registrar and Maureen. The list had been heavy and he leaned now against the radiator, listening to Maureen and Sister chatting idly while they drank their coffee. Presently he would go and see his patients, give instructions to the faithful registrar and

take himself off home. Hopefully the weekend would
be free of emergencies and he could take his ease.
And go and see Katrina.

The phone rang and Sister answered it and handed
the phone to Maureen. 'For you, Miss Soames, an
outside call.'

Whoever it was had a great deal to say, and
Maureen's face, from one of polite enquiry, turned
to concern.

She kept that look on her face while she thought
rapidly. She didn't waste much thought on the fire,
or her aunt's concern—the damage didn't sound too
bad and no one was hurt—but she saw at once how
she could turn it to her advantage. She lifted eyes
brimming with tears to Sister. 'My aunt's house is
on fire. She's safe but they're trying to save the furniture. She's distraught and there's no one there—no
family.' She turned back to the phone. 'I'm coming,
Auntie,' she said, in a voice shaky enough to arouse
sympathy in her companions. 'Just as soon as I can.'

She put down the receiver and turned to the professor. 'I must go to her, sir. I'm on call for the
weekend, I know, but if someone could take over just
while I go and see what's happening, I'll come back
the moment I've made sure that my aunt will be all
right.'

'Of course you must go. Your aunt has friends to
whom she might go if she needs to?'

'Yes, yes, of course. But at the weekend so many
of them are away.' That sounded feeble even in her
ears; there were any number of people in the village
willing to help in a time of need. She managed to
squeeze out a tear and gave a small sob which she
bravely choked back.

A splendid performance, thought the registrar sourly, and watched Sister sigh with sympathy. He watched the professor too, waiting.

'I'll drive you down.' The professor glanced at his watch. 'If need be you can stay there overnight and come back here as soon as possible on Sunday.'

Maureen made a show of hesitating. 'But I'm upsetting your weekend, and someone will have to stand in for me.'

The professor put down his mug. 'Go and get ready. I'll be at the entrance in twenty minutes or so. I'll see about your replacement.'

Maureen smiled bravely. 'Oh, thank you. I'm so very grateful.'

What a chance, she reflected as she changed into a linen two-piece the colour of her eyes and went to work on her face. Once they were there she must contrive to keep him there for as long as possible— overnight, perhaps. She stuffed things into a shoulder bag and went down to the entrance.

She had kept him waiting for more than ten minutes, but he said nothing, only ushered her into the car and drove off, listening with half an ear as she enlarged about her aunt's phone call while he thought about Katrina. He would take Maureen to the Manor and then go and see Katrina. It was still only late afternoon; they would have the evening together, and on Sunday he would fetch her to spend the day at his home. It's an ill wind, he thought, and wished that Maureen would stop talking.

But it was too good an opportunity to be missed, and she exerted all her charm, contriving to give the impression of a girl who, however good she was at her job, still needed the care and protection of a man...

When they arrived at the Manor the fire was smouldering, but contained. Half the village were there, running to and fro, carrying out rugs and furniture in danger of being damaged by water and smoke. Lady Truscott was sitting beside the sweep before the house, and the professor could see that she was by no means without help and comfort; he hadn't realized that Maureen was so devoted to her. He parked the car and they went over to speak to her.

She began to talk at once, but Maureen interrupted her. 'Aunt, Professor Glenville drove me down. I'm sure you can offer him dinner and have him stay the night...?'

Before she could reply, the professor said, in a voice which would brook no argument, 'Thank you, but I must return at once. I'm glad to see that you are unhurt and being looked after, Lady Truscott.' He turned to Maureen. 'You'll come back on duty as soon as you can?' He glanced round him. 'There are plenty of helpers; I see they are already beginning to take things back inside the house.'

He wished them goodbye and went back to his car. On his way he stopped several times, asking the same question: had Miss Gibbs been seen there, and if so was she still in the house, helping?

It was only when he questioned a fourth man that he had his answer.

'Miss Katrina? She's been here, all right. The first to come, so I hear. She got things organised a bit—went back in to pull a boy out of the place too. Gone 'ome, she 'as. Looked fair done up, too.'

The professor thanked him, got into his car and drove to Rose Cottage. He went up the path to its half-open door and went in without knocking.

There was no one in the living room, but Katrina was in the kitchen, sitting at the table. She was smoke-grimed, with a dirty face, the heirloom cloth still on the top of her bedraggled hair. Her dress was singed and there were scratches on her arms. Not a pretty sight, and yet to the professor she was all that was most beautiful.

She looked up as he went in. She said the first thing which entered her head.

'Would you feed Betsy? There's a tin...'

He saw to the little cat's needs without fuss, then he came to the table, plucked her gently from her chair and held her close. 'Are you hurt?'

Her voice was muffled by his shoulder. 'No, just scratched a bit—so silly!'

She was weeping now, and he let her sob and sniff for a few minutes, then said, 'Go and have a warm bath. Don't bother to dress again. I'll put on the kettle, and we'll have a cup of tea together and you shall tell me exactly what happened.'

He sounded soothing and kind, like an uncle or a big brother, she thought confusedly, and when he said, 'Run along now,' she went upstairs and had a bath and washed her hair. Presently she went back downstairs, smelling of shampoo and soap and wrapped in a dressing gown—a useful garment totally without glamour.

The professor had made the tea. He had made a plate of buttered toast too and set it tidily on the table. He pulled out a chair for her and moved around the kitchen as though he had lived there all his life, opening cupboards until he found a pot of jam. He put that on the table too, and sat down opposite her, pouring the tea and putting toast on a plate for her. He hadn't said anything but his silence was restful, and she had the feeling that she was wrapped around by caring comfort. She took a sip of tea.

'I'm sorry you walked into such a mess,' she said. 'I was a bit tired... Did you know that there had been a fire at the Manor?'

'Yes, nothing too serious, I understand, and plenty of help. How came you to be there?'

He offered her the toast, took a piece himself and took a large bite.

She told him about it in a matter-of-fact way. 'Of course it was awkward as Lady Truscott was in the bath and had no one there but her maid and the butler. I'm glad the damage wasn't too great; it's such a nice old house.'

They had more tea and he got up and came round to sit on the table beside her. 'I'll take a look at those scratches. You weren't burnt at all? Didn't breathe in any smoke?'

'They're only small scratches. I did get a few mouthfuls of smoke but I was sick on the way back here. I feel better now.'

'And the boy you pulled out of the passage, was he all right?'

'Oh, how did you know about him? I think he was all right; he was breathing normally and someone was looking after him.' She frowned. 'Perhaps I should have stayed...'

'It was brave of you to haul him out. You could just as easily have shouted to one of the men to go after him.'

'Oh, yes, well, I didn't think of that.'

He smiled. 'No, I don't suppose you did. Don't move; I'm going to see to the worst of the scratches.'

He had brought his bag in with him and he dealt with her small hurts and bruises.

'Do I still smell smoky?' asked Katrina.

Her still damp hair got in his way and he drew it aside. She smelled sweet, like a small child, he thought. He said quietly, 'No, not so much as a whiff.'

He wanted very much to sweep her into his arms and kiss her, but, Katrina being Katrina, he knew that would be a mistake. He went back to his side of the table.

'Now that Mrs Ward and Tracey have gone I expect you are able to enjoy a social life?'

He spoke casually, friendly and impersonal, so that she felt at ease with him and answered him readily.

'Well, I see more of my friends—tennis mostly—and of course I see Dr Peters and his wife quite often…'

'No dining and dancing?' he asked lightly.

'No.' And in case he should feel sorry for her she added, 'There's a lot to do in the garden at this time of year.' Wishful to change the subject, she asked, 'Have you come to see Dr Peters? Mrs Peters was saying the other day that she hoped you would go and see them when you were free.'

'I drove Maureen Soames down. She had a phone call from her aunt. She was very upset to hear about the fire and felt that she must be with her. In fact the situation isn't as bad as they thought it would be, and since she's on duty this weekend there's no need for her to stay here.'

There was ice spreading in Katrina's insides where there had been a comfortable glow from the professor's presence. She said in a stiff little voice, 'It must have been upsetting news for her. I'm sure Lady Truscott was glad to see her. It was very kind of you to come and see me. I hope your evening hasn't been spoilt. Don't let me keep you from what there is left of it.'

The professor frowned, hearing the sudden change in her voice. Katrina had pokered up and he wondered why. Probably she was tired and was longing for her bed. Obviously she wished him gone.

He took the mugs to the sink, saying casually, 'Well, I'll be off. A good night's sleep will put you back to rights. Take care of yourself, Katrina.'

She had the feeling that perhaps she had dismissed him too abruptly.

'You're going back to London this evening?'

'My dear girl, you should know by now we medical men and women are always ready to answer the call of duty.'

His smile was mocking. He added, 'Don't get up, I'll see myself out. Take care of yourself.'

Driving back to London, he reflected that he was making no progress with Katrina; he was too old for her, and what he had hoped would become a warm friendship, and even more than that, hadn't materialised. He had made it plain to her that he had fallen in love with her but had no intention of doing more about it until she was ready. And she had been happy about that, he was quite sure—but now perhaps she had had second thoughts. He had no intention of giving up. He would give her a few days and then go and see her again. He loved her, and he felt in his bones that hidden in her heart was her love for him.

Katrina went to bed, conscious of the emptiness now that Simon had gone. Somehow or other she must find a way of stopping him from coming to see her. He was doing it from kindness, but his visits merely served to make it harder for her to forget him. She had thought after their day together that he was letting her see that he had fallen in love with her, but she must have been mistaken.

'Wishful thinking,' she told Betsy, making ready for church in the morning.

There were rather more people in church than usual, not so much to give thanks for the saving of the Manor House from destruction as to glean any interesting details about it from other members of the congregation. After the service, progress from the church and through the churchyard was slow while those with snippets of information imparted them to friends. Lady Truscott had been in church, and so, to Katrina's surprise, had Maureen. Surely she should have gone back with Simon? Not that it was any business of hers, Katrina told herself loftily, making her way through the porch, to be stopped by the vicar.

'Katrina, I hear that you acted with your usual good sense yesterday. I'm sure that Lady Truscott must feel most grateful, Ah, here she is, no doubt to echo my words.'

Lady Truscott was rather enjoying herself. She wasn't exactly a heroine, but she was certainly a figure of interest for the whole village. She said as she joined Katrina and the vicar, 'My dear, I wanted to see you and thank you. From all accounts you were splendid, organising things. Such a pity that I was in my bath.' She gave a trill of laughter. 'And fire or no fire I had to get dressed, otherwise I would have been on the spot to organise things myself. So sensible of you to get the silver and the pictures out of the house.' She patted Katrina's arm. 'You're dear aunt all over again, my dear.'

Maureen had joined them. She and Katrina exchanged hellos, and Katrina saw the dislike in the other girl's eyes.

'I'm not supposed to be here,' she said. 'Professor Glenville drove me down yesterday. He wanted me to go back with him but I begged him to let me stay. He's so understanding, isn't he? He'll come for me later today—he wanted to be here with me but he simply had to return.'

'Travelling is difficult on a Sunday, isn't it?' said Katrina politely. 'But I expect there was someone to take your place if you were supposed to be on duty.' She smiled sweetly. 'No one is indispensable, are they?'

'That hardly applies to the medical profession,' said Maureen coldly. 'I suppose you're at a loose end now that child has gone? You must get bored. Haven't you got a job?'

'I start in September...'

'Oh, yes, Simon told me something about it. Anything's better than staying at home turning into a dried-up old spinster.' She added with a sneer, 'Though I suppose there are plenty of suitable men you could marry.'

Katrina kept her temper. 'Why, yes, I dare say there are, but I'm very happy as I am. Twenty-four isn't all that old. If I were getting close to thirty I might begin to worry…!'

She remembered that Maureen was twenty-nine; Lady Truscott had let that slip one day. She had scored a bull's-eye and Maureen's mouth looked ugly.

Lady Truscott had finished her gossip with Mrs Peters and the vicar and she said brightly, 'Are you two girls having a nice chat? I'm sure you must have a great deal in common.'

Katrina thought, Yes, *Simon*, but she didn't say so, only took a civil leave of Lady Truscott and Maureen and walked to where Dr Peters was waiting with the car. Mrs Peters had insisted that she went back with them for lunch, for that lady wanted a blow-by-blow account of the fire.

'Lady Truscott is so vague,' she told Katrina. 'A dear soul, but never gets anything right, if you see what I mean. And fancy being in the bath…! And only that dull-witted maid of hers there.'

So Katrina had to recount the excitements of the previous day, and when she had finished Mrs Peters said, 'You went home alone? You poor girl, you must have been tired and awfully dirty by then. Someone should have gone with you.'

'Well, Professor Glenville called and made tea while I got cleaned up.'

Dr Peters speared a roast potato. 'He drove Maureen Soames down, I'm told. She seems to have got him under her thumb. Her aunt told me that she was actually on duty at the hospital but she coaxed him into bringing her.'

He shot Katrina a quick glance, but she said nothing. However, his wife observed, 'I should have thought he was the last man in the world to be coaxed into doing something unless he wanted to do it. Still, if her aunt is to be believed, they're as good as engaged.'

She helped herself to horseradish sauce. 'She'll lead him a dance...'

'I believe she's good at her job,' said the doctor. 'Talking of jobs, when do you start at the library, Katrina?'

The talk was back on safe ground. Katrina enlarged upon the prospect of a career at the library, and presently the doctor drove her back home.

Alone, she changed into an old dress, got into sandals and went into the garden. It was very warm; there had been no rain for some days now and everything would need watering. It took some time, going to and fro with the watering can, and she was glad to sit down with the tea tray and Betsy for company. She had promised herself that she wouldn't think about Simon, but of course she did.

So he had told Maureen that she had found a job—how dared he discuss her with the wretched girl, as though she were someone to be pitied? Perhaps he did pity her. Perhaps he had told her that he had fallen in love with her just to cheer her up—something said on the spur of the moment and which he was probably regretting. He had been kind and warmly friendly yesterday, but given the circumstances anyone would have behaved in a similar manner.

And he had left abruptly.

She must forget him, contrive never to see him again. She has misunderstood him; he had wanted to cheer her up and he had said the first thing which entered his head... A nonsensical idea, but she told herself it was the answer.

She went to bed presently, telling herself that tomorrow was the beginning of another week—a week in which she would begin, too, to forget him.

Halfway through the week the weather changed with dramatic suddenness. The hot day was enveloped in black clouds with a nasty yellow tinge to them. They were in for a storm.

Katrina hurried round the garden, picking the fruit before it should be ruined by rain, tidying away the garden tools in the shed, covering the potatoes she had dug with an old sack. The first great drops were falling as she reached the porch, and a flash of lightning sent her inside with the door shut. She was scared of storms, and so was Betsy; they looked at each other, thankful that they had each other for company.

The storm had come to stay. It rumbled into the distance, then returned with even more noise and vivid lightning. Katrina made tea, and when the lights began to flicker prudently found candles. She was frightened now. Betsy had hidden herself in a corner and Katrina was sitting in a chair facing the door when it was opened. The professor, a vast figure outlined by a flash of lightning, stood there.

# CHAPTER NINE

KATRINA, who never screamed, screamed now. It wasn't a very loud scream, and it was drowned by the cracking thunder overhead, but next moment the professor was beside her, a large arm flung round her shoulders. He was very wet, and Barker and Jones, wreathing themselves around her legs, were even wetter, but that didn't matter. She buried her face against his vast reassuring chest, her eyes tight shut against the next flash of lightning.

Even with her eyes shut it was terrifyingly vivid, and the noise of the thunder made speech useless. The silence which followed was uncanny. She opened a cautious eye and the professor said cheerfully, 'Hello, have you any candles? I think we might need them.'

'There's one on the table.' She flinched at another flash of lightning.

He took one arm away. 'Then we'll light it together. Are there any more?'

'Yes. Two on the shelf by the door.'

He was lighting the candle when the lights went out. 'Just in time,' he observed. 'Let's have a cup of tea.'

She drew away from him reluctantly. 'There's a towel hanging on the door, if you want to dry yourself and Barker and Jones. I'll get more towels...'

He popped her into a chair. 'Sit there. We won't

go away, and probably the worst of the storm is over.'

He put the kettle on, dried his face and then towelled the dogs, fetched mugs and milk and made the tea. 'You're very handy around the house,' said Katrina, and let out a squeak at another vivid flash.

'I have a very loving mother and I had a fierce old-fashioned nanny. They both made sure that I would be capable of cherishing a wife in the proper manner, so that meant making a cup of tea, doing the washing up and offering a shoulder to cry on.'

He put a mug of tea on the table beside her and sat down. The candlelight was soft and dim. He studied her pale face and thought how beautiful she was.

'Your mother,' said Katrina. 'And your father?'

'Retired now. An orthopaedic surgeon. They live in a village near Huntingdon. I was born there.' He smiled at her over his mug. 'I have two sisters and a young brother. My sisters are married; Nick, at the moment, is heart-whole.'

'A family,' said Katrina wistfully, and gave a squeaky, 'Oh,' at a particularly loud clap of thunder. And then, unable to prevent her tongue from uttering, she said, 'I expect you're visiting at the Manor with Maureen.'

The professor put his mug down, putting two and two together at last. He said quietly, 'No, and certainly not with Maureen. I came to see you, Katrina. But first of all tell me why you supposed that I would be at the Manor with Maureen?'

He was smiling a little but he was staring at her hard. She looked away, because it would be easier to talk if she didn't look at him.

'Well,' she began, 'Lady Truscott said that you

and Maureen… And Maureen told me… Oh, does it matter?'

'Very much! Go on.'

'She talked as though you were going to marry her.' She glanced at his face and then met eyes like blue ice.

'And you believed her? Even after I had told you that I had fallen in love with you?'

He sounded so mild that she was emboldened to continue. 'Well, I didn't want to, only I thought she's such a suitable wife for you. I mean, you have to think of your future; you'll get more and more well-known, and meet all the right kinds of people. Not someone like me, grubbing around in the garden and doing the church flowers and making ends meet.'

'My darling girl, there is nothing I should enjoy more than grubbing in the garden with you; you may do all the church flowers you wish and we will make sure that ends always meet!'

'You don't want to marry Maureen?'

'No. I want to marry you, Katrina. But I have been waiting for you to be sure that you want to marry me. Rid your head of this nonsense about Maureen and think about us. And when you are quite sure of what you want, tell me.'

When she would have spoken, he said, 'No, my dear, give yourself time—only remember that I love you.' He became suddenly brisk. 'You need to go to your room and pack a bag. I'll come with you with a candle.'

'A bag? Why do I need to pack a bag?'

He glanced at his watch. 'We can be in Huntingdon in three hours. You will like my mother, I think, and she very much wants to meet you.'

At Katrina's surprised look, he added, 'Oh, she knows all about you.'

He was on his feet, holding a candle. 'Come on, pack enough for a few days. If you need anything I'm sure someone will lend you whatever it is.'

He was propelling her towards the stairs. 'And has Betsy a basket, or shall I find a box?'

'A basket. It's in the cupboard under the sink.' Katrina turned round on the stairs and said earnestly, 'But, Simon, I can't. I don't know your mother and there's a dreadful storm and I'm frightened.'

He smiled at her very tenderly. 'When I am with you are you frightened, Katrina?'

She said breathlessly, 'No—no, I'm not.'

'Good.' He put the candlestick down. 'I'm going to get Betsy's basket and see to the windows and doors. If you are frightened I'll come up at once.'

Katrina told herself that she was in a dream and would wake up presently, but that didn't prevent her packing an overnight bag. She did this in a slapdash fashion which would have shocked Aunt Thirza, before tearing out of the cotton frock she had been wearing in the garden and getting into a cotton jersey dress and jacket. There was no time to do her hair. She brushed it back fiercely, thrust a pair of shoes on top of the contents of the bag and turned round just as the professor reached the small landing.

'Good girl! Betsy's in her basket. I fed her first.' His gaze raked her. 'You look nice.'

Katrina went pink under the look. 'My dressing gown,' she said breathlessly.

'That's something you can borrow. But bring a mac if you have one.'

The storm was dying away and the rain was easing

off at last. The sky was a uniform grey, but inside the Bentley it was warm and comfortable. With the dogs and Betsy in the back and her bag in the boot they drove away from Rose Cottage.

They didn't talk much, and Katrina was glad of that; she had a great deal to think about for her thoughts were in a hopeless muddle. Presently she gave up and settled back into her seat, allowing herself to feel nothing but happiness.

For all the world as if she had spoken her thoughts out loud, the professor said in a soothing voice, 'Don't tease your head with doubts and fancies, my darling. You trust me, don't you?'

'Yes, Simon, of course I do…'

'Tomorrow, when you've had a good night's sleep, we will talk. Are you comfortable? And warm enough? I'm going up on the A303, then onto the M25 and north to Huntingdon. We'll stop halfway for coffee. We shall be there some time before eleven o'clock.'

There was very little traffic, and the Bentley swept along at a speed which made light of the miles. They stopped at a service station just before they joined the M25, walked the dogs and made sure that Betsy was quiet in her basket, and had coffee. When they got back into the car the professor picked up the phone and talked to his mother, dropped a kiss on Katrina's cheek and drove on.

The clocks were striking half past ten as they drove through Huntingdon and took the road to the village of Brampton, silent and dimly lighted now, and then on to Buckden, its wide high street flanked by facing inns, the houses mostly Georgian and Jacobean. At the far end of the village Simon turned the car into a narrow lane which ended at a wide-open gateway. The drive leading to the house was short, and since most of the downstairs windows were lighted Katrina had time to get a glimpse of the house. Brick, Jacobean and of a comfortable size, with, as far as she could see, wide lawns and flowerbeds around it.

The front door was flung open as he stopped the car and an elderly Labrador loped out, barking, followed by an elderly man.

Simon got out, opened Katrina's door, let the dogs out and took her arm. 'I'll get Betsy in a moment.' He shook hands with his father. 'Katrina, this is my father—Father, your future daughter-in-law.'

Her hand was grasped and she was kissed warmly. 'My dear girl, we are so happy to have you here. Come inside. You're not too tired to meet everyone?'

The hall was square and panelled in a dark wood and seemed full of people.

The professor had her hand now, and led her to a grey-haired woman, very upright with a pretty smiling face. He bent to kiss her and said simply, 'Here she is Mother. Katrina, this is my mother.'

Mrs Glenville gave her a warm kiss. 'My dear, we are so delighted. Can you bear to come into the drawing room and meet the rest of the family?'

She led the way into the drawing room and everyone followed her, to surround Katrina and Simon—his sisters and his brother, shaking hands and kissing her and declaring how delighted they were.

'And we simply had to come here to welcome you,' said Miriam, the elder sister. 'You must be tired after that drive. We won't stay. Donald and I live in Huntingdon and Becky and John live in

Cambridge, and of course Nick's at the hospital there. We're all coming over for lunch tomorrow, but we couldn't wait…'

They left presently, and Katrina was sat down and plied with coffee and sandwiches, watched over by her future mother-in-law and a small stout woman, Dolly, the housekeeper. Katrina ate and drank obediently, and in between answered Mrs Glenville's kindly questions and looked around her.

The room was large, with tall narrow windows draped in heavy velvet curtains. It was panelled, like the hall, and there were rugs on the wooden floor. There were Georgian wing armchairs and two magnificent sofas, buttoned and covered in the same rich wine-red of the curtains, and a number of small tables were scattered round. There was a walnut bureau cabinet against one wall, and a glass-fronted display cabinet facing it, and a brass lantern clock above the marble fireplace. A lovely, lived-in room.

'Tomorrow, if Simon will spare you for an hour, we will go round the house,' said Mrs Glenville comfortably. 'And now you are to go to bed, my dear.'

Simon had been standing by the window, watching the dogs outside, talking to his father. He crossed the room as his mother spoke.

'Your room has a balcony. You'd like to have Betsy with you, wouldn't you?'

The small thoughtful kindness brought unexpected tears to Katrina's eyes. 'You don't mind? She'll be good…'

'My dear,' declared Mrs Glenville, 'cats and dogs wander all over this house, and when the boys were young we had tame rats as well.'

She kissed Katrina. 'Sleep well, Katrina. I'll come to your room with you.'

Simon's father bade her goodnight too, and Simon went to the door to open it. His mother went past him with a smile, but he caught Katrina in a vast hug and kissed her soundly. She kissed him back, which encouraged him to kiss her again. 'Goodnight, my love, my very dear love.'

She treasured the words as she followed Mrs Glenville upstairs to the wide landing. Mrs Glenville opened a door. 'Dolly will have put your things away, dear. Your bathroom's next door, and if you want anything do ask. I'm sure you came away in a hurry.'

The room was pretty; when Mrs Glenville had gone Katrina wandered round admiring the chintz curtains and the bedspread, the thick carpet underfoot and the little pink lamps each side of the bed. The furniture was of some light wood, and someone had thoughtfully laid out brush and comb, hairpins and hairspray. The balcony was small, and she found Betsy there, sitting in her basket in a composed fashion. Someone had fed her, for there was a saucer by her. Katrina marvelled at the thoughtfulness of her hostess, and at a moment's notice too.

She undressed then, and had a bath in the small bathroom leading from her room. And although someone had unpacked her toothbrush and soap, and anything else she had swept into her sponge bag at a moment's notice, there were enough soaps and lotions and bath luxuries there to keep her happy for a week.

She got into bed finally, determined to go over the day's happenings in a sensible way. She was blissfully happy, but she must remember to be practical as well... Betsy crept onto the bed and curled up beside her, and Katrina, despite her good resolutions, went to sleep too.

She woke when a young girl in a very clean print apron drew back the curtains and put a tray of tea on the table beside the bed with a cheerful good morning. 'And Mr Simon says he'll be at the front door in twenty minutes, miss.'

Wide awake now, Katrina drank her tea, offered a saucer of milk to Betsy and jumped out of bed. She had a quick shower and dressed. She put on a cotton dress, wishing she had had more time to select the best of her wardrobe, pinned up her hair in a hurry, put on her sandals, begged Betsy to be good and flew downstairs.

Simon was standing at the open door with the dogs beside him. He came to meet her as she crossed the hall, put his hands on her shoulders and looked down into her happy face.

'You slept well? Perhaps I should have left you to sleep longer.'

He didn't kiss her, and after a moment she said, 'I slept very well, and I couldn't stay in bed on such a glorious morning. Are we going for a walk?'

When he nodded, she set off beside him; she had expected to be kissed, but his greeting had been casual. Perhaps now that she was at his family home—away from Rose Cottage—he was having second thoughts...

They walked the length of the big garden behind the house, crossed a plank bridge over the small stream at the end of it and began a gentle climb through the trees of a copse which covered the low

hill before them. The path was narrow. Simon led
the way, extending a hand behind him to hold hers,
and as she felt his firm cool grip her silly fears became nonsense.

At the top of the hill the trees petered out onto a
flat grassy patch overlooking the country before
them: a pleasant vista of fields, with the last of the
wheat being harvested, cows and horses roaming
here and there, and in the distance a winding river.
And over it all the sun shone from a blue sky.

Still holding hands, they stood and looked, and
Katrina said, 'It's so glorious…no one minds us being here?'

'No—it belongs to the family. It's a place I love
and that's why we've come here together, because
this is where I'm asking you to marry me, Katrina.'

She turned into his arms as naturally as a child.
'Oh, Simon, there's nothing I want more, and, yes,
please, I'll marry you.'

He bent to kiss her, and she knew then why he
hadn't kissed her that morning. There was no need
for him to speak, the kiss told her everything.
Presently she lifted her head. 'You never seemed to
be in love with me.'

'My dearest, I have been so frightened of scaring
you away. I think I've loved you from the moment
I saw you sprawling in the road—and so cross too.'

He kissed her again. 'And so delightful and so
aloof. Your hidden heart tucked away out of sight
for fear of anyone discovering how lonely you were.'
His arm tightened around her.

'I had Aunt Thirza.'

'A wonderful lady; she was your mother and father, brothers and sisters, and she loved you. And

now you have another family.' He added, suddenly brisk, 'We had better go and eat our breakfast with them...'

They stayed for three days, and when they drove back to Rose Cottage the plans for their wedding had been made—in just over a month's time, after the banns had been read, and in the village church. And it was to be a white wedding.

Katrina, dreaming of white silk and orange blossom had said, 'And I'd like Tracey to be my bridesmaid.' She had sat down and written a letter straight away, while the Glenville family made a list of guests.

It was a formidable list. 'But I haven't any family,' Katrina had said.

'The Peterses, Mrs Ward, Lady Truscott—half the village,' Simon had reminded her.

They had left directly after an early breakfast and were back at Rose Cottage by midday. Simon didn't delay long, he had private patients to see later that afternoon, but they had brought a picnic with them and sat down in the kitchen to eat it while the dogs and Betsy roamed round the garden.

'I won't be able to see much of you, darling, for the next week or two. I'll come down on Sunday and hear the banns read, but I'll be in Bristol on the following week.' He glanced at his watch. 'We just have time to see your vicar. He'll have had my letter, so it shouldn't take more than a few minutes.'

An hour later Katrina was back at the cottage. The banns had been arranged and Simon had kissed her goodbye and driven away. She would have to get used to that, she reflected soberly; doctors had to share their lives with so many other people. But he would always come back to her... She smiled widely as she tidied the kitchen.

Simon's mother had wasted no time. The invitation cards had been printed while they were at Simon's home, and Katrina got them out of her bag now and started making a list. Tomorrow she would go to Mrs Dyer's and post them. She sat up late, making more lists; she would need clothes, a wedding dress and a veil, a dress for Tracey, a new wardrobe, however small, in which to start married life...

The village was agog. It was to be the wedding of the year; best hats were taken from their boxes and refurbished, flowers for the church promised from all sides, and Mrs Dyer and a party of chosen ladies went off to Warminster to choose a suitable present for the happy pair. Lady Truscott offered the Manor for the reception, Dr Peters begged to be allowed to give Katrina away, and Mrs Ward wrote to say that Tracey was over the moon and could she have a pink dress?

And there had been a great bunch of red roses from Simon.

Sunday came and Katrina got up far too early, anxious to be ready for Simon. There was so much to tell him. When he did come she flew into his arms. Never mind all the plans to be discussed, they could wait for a while.

He looked tired, she thought anxiously, but there was nothing tired in his greeting. 'We'll go home for the rest of the day,' he told her. 'Mrs Peach has been up half the night cooking something special. Have we time for coffee?'

She had it ready, and they sat at the kitchen table opposite each other.

'Now tell me your news,' he invited, and then grinned suddenly. 'It's hard to be sensible, isn't it?'

She put out a hand and he took it in his. She said, suddenly shy, 'Yes, it is.' And then she began on her news. 'Everyone has been so kind. Dr Peters wants to give me away, I've booked rooms for your family at the Dog and Thistle—it's quite comfortable and very clean. I hope it will do—and Lady Truscott wants us to have the reception at the Manor. It's her wedding present to us. Only I said I must ask you first. The whole village has been invited.'

'So we had better accept, hadn't we?' He smiled and said, 'And don't worry that Maureen will be there. She left yesterday. She's taken a sudden vacancy in a team going to India. The hospital released her on the grounds of urgency.'

He leaned across the table and kissed her. 'I've missed you, my dear love. And I shall be away until next weekend. But I've brought a phone with me, so at least we can talk each evening. I shall have to go straight to St Aldrick's on Saturday, when I get back, but I'll be here on Sunday and this time we'll go to *my* church and hear the banns read there.'

He put down his mug. 'And I've something else.' He took a small box from his pocket and opened it. The ring was old-fashioned, three sapphires set in diamonds, and it was beautiful. 'It was my grandmother's.'

He took her hand and slipped the ring on her finger and she said. 'It's beautiful, Simon. I'll wear it with pride and love.'

He picked up her hand and kissed the palm. 'We

have to go together and get our wedding rings. Not next week, of course, but I'll keep a day free after that.'

And presently they went to church and sat, unmindful of the friendly stares, and heard their banns read.

Katrina went to London that week, taking with her all the money she had. She must have a wedding dress, and a pretty outfit in which to go away, then one or two new dresses, and she also needed shoes and undies—a whole host of things she had managed to do without. And of course pink silk for Tracey's dress.

She spent the whole day going from one shop to the next and went home laden with parcels, well pleased with herself. The wedding dress she had discovered after a dedicated search—cream chiffon over a silk slip, very plain, with long sleeves and a modest neckline. She had found it in a small shop off Oxford Street, and the saleswoman had found a delicate veil to go with it. After that she had patiently tracked down almost everything else she needed, and there was still a little money left.

She set to work the next day on Tracey's dress, with its matching cap, and what with her sewing and people calling with good wishes and presents the week flew by. And each evening Simon phoned her.

On the following Sunday he came, and they drove to Wherwell, went to church and then spent the day in the garden with the dogs, exchanging their news, pausing now and then to smile at each other, two people quite sure of their love. The professor drove her back to Rose Cottage in the late evening, bidding her a most satisfying goodbye and telling her that he would fetch her early the next day so that they might buy their wedding rings...

And then, suddenly, it was her wedding day. Mrs Ward and Tracey had arrived the day before, and were to stay until Katrina and Simon got back from their honeymoon and could collect Betsy. They were up early, and presently Mrs Ward and Tracey left for the church and Katrina was alone, sitting quietly waiting for Dr Peters.

She looked beautiful in her pretty dress, her bouquet laid carefully on the table. Simon had sent it: white roses with creamy hearts, lilies, orange blossom and stephanotis and, tucked into its heart, moss roses. She sniffed their freshness and wished that Aunt Thirza could have been with her, but it wasn't a day to feel sad, and she looked up with a small smile as Dr Peters came up the path to fetch her.

The church was packed, and those who couldn't get in were waiting outside to see Katrina arrive. For a moment she hesitated in the porch. The sea of faces under festive hats were turned towards her, and then she didn't see them any more. There was Simon, her dear professor, immaculate in his morning coat. If only he would turn around...

He did, and smiled down the length of the aisle to her, and she smiled back as she and the doctor began to walk towards him. The church might be filled with people, but for the two of them there was no one else there, only the vicar reciting the age-old ceremony.

It wasn't until they were at the Manor, awaiting the first of their guests, that the professor took her by the hand and led her to a small room off the entrance hall.

'Why are we here?' asked Katrina. 'Everyone's

coming through the front door.' She tugged at his arm. 'Simon, dear…'

He took her gently in his arms. 'They won't be here for a minute or two, and in that time I can kiss my wife.'

Which he did, with a thoroughness that betokened well for their future happiness.

Katrina tucked her veil out of the way. 'If this is being married then I'm going to like it very much,' she told him.

He kissed her finally, rearranged her veil, and a moment later there they were, smiling calmly at the first of their guests. Professor and Mrs Glenville.

# Harlequin Romance®

**brings you four very special weddings to
remember in our new series:**

*True love is worth waiting for....*

Look out for the following titles by some of
your favorite authors:

**August 1999—SHOTGUN BRIDEGROOM #3564**
**Day Leclaire**
Everyone is determined to protect Annie's good name and ensure
that bad boy Sam's seduction attempts don't end in the
bedroom—but begin with a wedding!

**September 1999—A WEDDING WORTH WAITING FOR #3569**
**Jessica Steele**
Karrie was smitten by boss Farne Maitland. But she was
determined to be a virgin bride. There was only one solution:
marry and quickly!

**October 1999—MARRYING MR. RIGHT #3573**
**Carolyn Greene**
Greg was wrongly arrested on his wedding night for something he
didn't do! Now he's about to reclaim his virgin bride when he dis-
covers Christina's intention to marry someone else....

**November 1999—AN INNOCENT BRIDE #3577**
**Betty Neels**
Katrina didn't know it yet but Simon Glenville, the wonderful doctor
who'd cared for her sick aunt, was in love with her. When the time
was right, he was going to propose....

*Available wherever Harlequin books are sold.*

# HARLEQUIN®
*Makes any time special.*™

Look us up on-line at: http://www.romance.net

HRWW

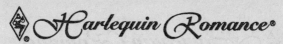

# Harlequin Romance®

We're proud to announce the "birth" of a brand-new series full of babies, bachelors and happy-ever-afters: *Daddy Boom*. Meet gorgeous heroes who are about to discover that there's a first time for everything—even fatherhood!

We'll be bringing you one deliciously cute *Daddy Boom* title every other month in 1999. Books in this series are:

**Who says bachelors and babies don't mix?**

Available wherever Harlequin books are sold.

# HARLEQUIN®
*Makes any time special.*™

# EXTRA! EXTRA!

**The book all your favorite authors
are raving about is finally here!**

**The 1999 Harlequin and Silhouette
coupon book.**

**Each page is alive with savings that can't be beat!**

**Getting this incredible coupon book is
as easy as 1, 2, 3.**

1. During the months of November and December 1999 buy any 2 Harlequin or Silhouette books.

2. Send us your name, address and 2 proofs of purchase (cash receipt) to the address below.

3. Harlequin will send you a coupon book worth $10.00 off future purchases of Harlequin or Silhouette books in 2000.

Send us 3 cash register receipts as proofs of purchase and we will send you 2 coupon books worth a total saving of $20.00 (limit of 2 books per customer).

**Saving money has never been this easy.**

Please allow 4-6 weeks for delivery. Offer expires December 31, 1999.

---

**I accept your offer! Please send me (a) coupon booklet(s):**

Name: _____

Address: _____  City: _____

State/Prov.: _____  Zip/Postal Code: _____

Send your name and address, along with your cash register receipts as proofs of purchase, to:

**In the U.S.:** Harlequin Books, P.O. Box 9057, Buffalo, N.Y. 14269

**In Canada:** Harlequin Books, P.O. Box 622, Fort Erie, Ontario L2A 5X3

Order your books and accept this coupon offer through our web site
http://www.romance.net
Valid in U.S. and Canada only.                         PHQ4994

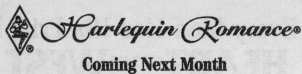

# Coming Next Month

**#3579 LONG-LOST BRIDE Day Leclaire**
Chaz found himself proposing to a beautiful mystery woman at the masked ball. She turned out to be Shayne—the woman he'd once loved more than life itself. They both needed to marry—but could Chaz ever truly forgive his long-lost bride?

*Fairytale Weddings: The Fairytale Weddings Ball: come single, leave wed!*

**#3580 A HUSBAND FOR CHRISTMAS Emma Richmond**
Gellis had begun to assume that Sebastien Fourcard had left her for another woman, when he returned—with amnesia! He couldn't remember loving Gellis, but he wanted to stay for the sake of their son. Gellis wanted his love—but not just for Christmas....

*Daddy Boom: Who says bachelors and babies don't mix?*

**#3581 KISSING SANTA Jessica Hart**
Amanda had to get Blair McAllister to sell his home to her company. But her plan to get close to him by taking the job of nanny to his three children backfired when she fell in love! Work forgotten, now all Amanda wanted was Blair—under the mistletoe....

**#3582 RESOLUTION: MARRIAGE Patricia Knoll**
Garrett Blackhawk is acting as if he never wrote to end his relationship with Mary Jane. He still wants her as his wife! Mary Jane is tempted, but forced to keep her distance. At least, until she's ready to share her secret—that her eldest daughter is also his!

*Marriage Ties: The four Kelleher women, bound together by family and love*